Alphonso Alva Hopkins

Our Sabbath Evening

Home Meditations

Alphonso Alva Hopkins

Our Sabbath Evening
Home Meditations

ISBN/EAN: 9783337371357

Printed in Europe, USA, Canada, Australia, Japan

Cover: Foto ©Andreas Hilbeck / pixelio.de

More available books at **www.hansebooks.com**

OUR

SABBATH EVENING:

HOME MEDITATIONS,

IN PROSE AND VERSE.

—BY—

ALPHONSO A. HOPKINS.

BOSTON:
D. LOTHROP & COMPANY,
32 FRANKLIN STREET.

CONTENTS.

TO

MY MOTHER,

THE   HUMAN   INSPIRATION

OF

WHATEVER   IS   TRUE   AND   WORTHY   IN   MY   LIFE,

AND   OF

ALL   THAT   IS   PUREST   AND   MOST   HELPFUL

IN   MY   WRITINGS ;

AND   TO

MY   PASTOR,

ABOUT   WHOSE   MORNING   THOUGHT

MY

EVENING   MEDITATIONS   OFTEN   CLUSTER,

I   DEDICATE

THIS   BOOK.

IN THE TWILIGHT.

SABBATH evenings are especially pleasant at home. However large or small the circle, an influence known at no other time through the week makes itself felt, and produces marked effects. Education has much to do with this, to be sure—and for the same let education be thanked! But there is a somewhat in the Sabbath atmosphere unlike anything in the week-day work and worry—a somewhat that is restful, and tranquillizing, and sweet. There is, or there ought to be. "Six days shalt thou labor," holds within it the truest economy of life, even considered wholly apart from any sacred significance. It is well for us at regular intervals to get away from our labor—to stand removed, as it were—and look upon it in the light of its relation to our inner existence—to walk out of our lower selves into a self that is higher, and better, and nobler.

We whose weeks are ever weeks of toil, need just what Sabbaths bring of quiet reflection. The world is a very busy world, and its opportunities for silent meditation are few, indeed. Amid its whirl and stir we are pressed upon every hand by duties that will not be thrust aside, and that too often call only our baser being into action.

Here in the home, as the Sabbath evening shadows gather, we have drifted out from the world, and all its discordant noises fade far away. The morning service—with its hymns that were in themselves a benediction, and its words that were a kindly ministry to our souls—the Bible-study that followed, and our afternoon's readings, have borne us outward, and only in our on-coming sleep need we drift back to the every-day being and doing (and sinning?) once more.

But though separate from the world for a little, we cannot forget its wants, its wickednesses, our own daily failures, our personal needs. The rather ought we to remember them in fervent prayer. The sermon of the morning had for its theme "The Resultant Effects of Sin ;" and the preacher showed by numerous illustrations that though we sorrow deeply over any transgressions our repentance cannot avert the natural consequence of such transgression. DAVID of old repented bitterly of his heinous sin before GOD, but the effects of that sin were not done away. "The child that is born unto thee shall surely die," was spoken in almost the same breath with that comforting assurance of pardon :—"The Lord also hath put away thy sin." So is it ever. GOD pardons the sin ; but its consequences remain. But for this we might go on sinning indefinitely, looking to a final repentance to clear it all away. In the light of this fact however, every added sin is a something added to the sum of evil consequences, forever beyond our reach, never to be effaced by repentance most sincere.

The world thinks differently, it would seem. Do we

not seem to think differently ourselves, often, when we mingle with the world? In the hush of our Sabbath evening we hear the heart's soft answer—"Yes." And we say to ourselves, in tenderly prayerful words—"Pray GOD that all sin may henceforth be kept far from us, so that none of its consequences shall be set down to our charge!" GOD grant to hear such petition, even as though it were addressed on bended knee!

THE NEW LEAF.

"WE have turned over a new leaf," said RUTH on New Year's morning.

"A new leaf!" How many are turned over with every New Year! It is a time for reflection, for fresh resolving, for added fervor of zeal.

Sitting here to-night, we look back over the old year, and seeing much that was base and impure, much of failure and faltering, we feel as though to turn over a new leaf were well indeed. We have so much to correct, so much to purify, so much to strengthen.

But does the turning over a new leaf once a year work out what is needed? Is it not a little sad to think so many new leaves must be turned over? What of the old ones? Are they full? and is the writing so crude and imperfect we blush over it? Or are they just blanks, or blanks in part, whereon we meant to write beautiful things and through waiting and hesitation failed to write at all?

Let us not quite give over the old leaves. If we held purposes noble and pure—and did we not?—let us hold to them still, with only a better endeavor, and a larger faith. If we planned well, but indolently neglected to execute, let us stand by the old plans. If our hope was a good hope, let us cherish it to the end. We may have newness of life, though we stand fast by the old year's purposing, planning, and hoping.

And it may be the new life in the old that shall bless us beyond measure. May be! Is there any doubt of it?

Our new life is always the old, with a difference. It is old—the individuality of it, the scope of it. Real newness came into it but once—when CHRIST's spirit gave the new impulse. Since then the only newness is a newness of doing. Shall the doing be really new and true in the year to come? Shall we write the new leaf full with steady purpose, with unfaltering faith, with love for GOD and our fellowmen?

> O would our leaves of life were fair
> With faithful writing everywhere!
> O would that love shone clear and true
> Each plan and purpose ever thro';
> That zeal did never faint and tire;
> That hope ne'er waned to low desire;
> That so each New Year's dawn should bring
> The old year's buds to blossoming,
> And so all hopes and plans should tend
> Through patient work to perfect end!

THE SILENT CHRIST.

ALONG Judea's homely ways
  The young Messiah trod,
Within Him hid through weary days
  The wonder-working God.

The sick no healing in Him knew,
  No help the smitten sore ;
To wretched Gentile, needy Jew,
  No aid divine He bore.

The blind went by Him to and fro,
  Through all their lonely night ;
Yet none the tender touch might know
  Of hands that held their sight.

The poor in poverty's distress
  Lay by the rich man's gate,
Nor dreamed that heavenly power to bless,
  Their faith could antedate.

Alone amid the mass of men
  He moved, the silent Christ,
To no divinest message, then,
  His human lips enticed.

A worker with the work day throng,
  Perhaps He yet could hear
Some strains of that transcendent song
  The angels chanted near ;

The sweet good-will, the peace on earth,
  With which they sung Him in,
Through lowly door of human birth,
  Upon the world of sin!

Perhaps He listened, rapt and still,
  Amid the noisy round,
To learn the Father's secret will,
  His purposes profound;

Perhaps upon Judea's sands
  He dreamed of waters sweet
That once He drank in heavenly lands
  Close by the Father's feet;

Perhaps upon Judea's hills
  He looked with longing eyes,
On scene no mortal vision thrills
  With tender, glad surprise;

Perhaps on lonely nights He slept
  To human sound and sense,
But waked to angels' touch and kept
  Their fit communion hence!

We may not know. He came and went
  With mortals, like the rest;
No hint of growing discontent
  His human life expressed;

From out His dual consciousness
  No word divine He spoke;
The silent Christ, in human dress,
  His silence never broke.

The world was weary grown indeed,
  And cried for Him in grief;

Around Him grew the human need,
And found no full relief.

And still He held His silent way—-
The waiting, silent Christ—
Till God's own long-appointed day
His lips to speech enticed !

Then whereso'er He chanced to be
He spake the Living Word ;
The hearts of men, the stormy sea,
In sudden wonder heard.

And ever since that blessed time
When silence found its speech,
In helpful syllables sublime
His words have come to each :

And never silence so divine
Shall walk the world again,
As lived and moved and made no sign,
Among Judea's men ;

As wrapped with human garb around,
The homely ways it trod,
And in its mystery profound
Was but the breath of God !

OVERCOMING.

RUTH was reading in Revelations, just before the twilight came on. When it grew too dark to see, we all sat there a while in silence.

"He that overcometh shall inherit all things," repeated RUTH, at last. "That is a blessed promise," she went on to say. "I think of no sweeter comfort for tired souls. And I am glad the phrase that precedes the promise is so comprehensive. 'He that overcometh; It does not say what must be overcome. It is not limited, in its application, to any particular individuality. It covers, so, all human stress and strain."

"Then you think each man and woman of us has somewhat to overcome?" one asked.

"I know it, "she responded, with feeling. "Life is a battle for us all. How hard the fight for some, you and I may never quite understand ; but it seems hard enough, even for us. We are borne down sometimes, to the very dust. We cry out with pain and longing. We want so much that we do not have—peace, and plenty, and luxury, the seeming joys of a richer and better endowed being than our own.

"What is it to overcome? Well, each one can answer that question for himself or herself. I believe in temptations according to temperament, and contests growing out of these peculiar to individual character. For me to overcome would be one thing; for you to overcome might be very different indeed. Is it not, primarily, just an overcoming of selfishness? So it seems, as I look at it. All that self wants only for self-satisfaction. and not self-improvement—that is to be battled against. Every passion that may degrade—that is to be conquered. Every desire and impulse that may work ill to the soul —these are to be set aside.

"And what is the gain? Much comes to us here, but the 'all things' of our inheritance who shall estimate? I like to feel that I *am to inherit*; that what is promised me I may not, can, not earn; that I must go out of this life poor as I entered it, whatever my service; that I am to be rich beyond measure by-and-by ju st because GOD is good beyond measure always, kind and tender and lovingly beneficent. His promise of an inheritance for me seals, somehow, my relation to Him. It makes me feel that He is truly my Father, and I am as t.uly His child. I shall not forever want, because His promises fail not. The infinite riches are certain, to such as are heirs of GOD."

WITH regard to the past—it is gone. Regrets are unavailing. And the future? It is not ours. We have the present, and that alone. Good resolutions for days to come are worth nothing. We must live as we would live, *now.*

DOUBTING DISCIPLES.

THE text of the preacher this morning was that remark of THOMAS, so heroic in form, so despondent in spirit— "Let us also go up, that we may die with him."

Was it merely a happen-so, that the small band of disciples chosen by our SAVIOUR numbered such diverse dispositions,—that there were so many distinct temperaments in it? Had not CHRIST a purpose in His every doing?—and were not these diverse natures chosen as so many types of what the vast army of disciples should be in years to come? We think so.

Thomas was the type of doubt. From all we can learn of him, he looked ever on the dark side of things; was continually prophesying evil to come. He was a sincere believer in the Master, perhaps, in the abstract. But he doubted in the detail. He felt uncertain of the end. He questioned always as to results.

How many of us so doubt, so question! Have we as good reason as had THOMAS? Assuredly not. It needed a stronger faith to believe unhesitatingly in JESUS CHRIST present in the flesh, than it now needs to believe in Him risen from the dead and sitting at the right hand of the Father. He was the carpenter's son, then; he has been our Mediator ever since. It is not so strange that THOMAS doubted then, as that Christians doubt to-day.

We know more of JESUS CHRIST than THOMAS knew, even after he put his hands in those gaping wounds. Christianity has been preaching its divine origin these 1,800 years,—preaching it with no additions, but with a more complete development. It has proved its character by what it has done for the race.

What excuse, therefore, have the doubting Thomases to-day? Suppose there are dark times in individual experience, why doubt? Suppose the end is hedged about and baffles our percievings, why despond? Such has been the case in thousands of other instances. Men have doubted, and desponded, but CHRIST lives yet. Uncertainty has brooded over all the way many times before, but we have always come out into clear paths after a while.

Verily, THOMAS was a type of what should be, but not of what ought to be. We may not shoulder all our dubious forecastings upon temperament, and hold ourselves blameless. As well might we excuse overt sin because we were born with a tendency to sinning. Men doubt, not so much because of any predisposition so to do, as because of a cultivated liking for unbelief. Men have cultured themselves into skepticism—they are doing it yet. Doubts will come to us, sometimes, and we are not to blame for their coming. But we are blameworthy if we let them take lodgment and stay,—if we feed and cherish them and let them invite others.

THE VALLEY OF ACHOR.

MAKE me to feel, O loving Son
   Of loving Father, just and kind,
That I with sin and doubt have done,
And now, with peace and trust at one,
   My will to Thee is all resigned !

Make me in fullest faith to see
   My every wickedness laid bare,
Renounced forever, as I flee
From this poor life of self, to Thee,
   And learn Thy love beyond compare !

Make this indeed to me the Vale
   Of Achor blest, where now I yield
The sweetest sin that would assail
My longing soul ; nor let me fail
   To show Thee, Lord, the sins concealed !

The wilderness through which I came
   Seems present yet ; but round me wait
The Canaan-lands, and in Thy name
I may possess them.   Mine the blame
   If for their sweets I famish late !

In weakness great, O Lord, I lift
   My face to Thee, in hunger sore !
Send still Thy manna sweet and swift,
And give my withered soul the thrill
   Of blessing gracious, I implore !

Here, Lord, I gladly give Thee all!
  My sins, my self, I yield to Thee!
Thou art not far from every call
Of burdened heart,—here let me fall
  Upon Thy breast, and burdens flee!

STRONG IN WEAKNESS.

"To suffer and grow strong." It is not the natural sequence. Suffering begets weakness, as a rule. Few suffer long and keep their vigor undiminished.

And we must all suffer. All? They are few who escape suffering. It comes to each in some form—suffering of the body, or mental anguish, or keen hurt of the soul. Does it come ever with a blessing? We know it does. We know that some characters find perfection through sorrow, even as CHRIST found His.

For was there not a progression in our SAVIOUR's life? He was tempted, and in many forms; did He not grow strong to resist temptation? Surely that final test was a hard one when He hung alone in the death agony, and His heart cried out so piteously after the Father. It was bad enough to be forgotten of men, and bruised for their iniquities; it was infinitely worse to be forsaken of GOD.

Through the suffering of sympathetic ministry, of the scorn of unbelievers, of long and bitter temptation, of agonizing prayer, of denial and betraying, of taunts and tortures, the Son of Man grew strong. Through suffering of some sort, the best strength must come to each of us. When out of suffering comes strength, then is suffering a blessing. How shall the strength come? The answer may be found in CHRIST's own life. He prayed much. He trusted ever in the Father and in the Father's love. In His prayers and His trust He grew strong. How else can men grow strong to-day?

A PRESENT CHRIST.

THE family circle had been some time quiet, as the shadows deepened. By-and-by a sweet voice stirred the silence, and we heard the tender strains of that touching little hymn—When Jesus Comes. It had a certain pathos in it for us all. Over the last stanza sung the singer lingered as if each word had peculiar comfort:

> "He'll know the way was dreary,
>   When Jesus comes;
> He'll know the feet grew weary,
>   When Jesus comes!"

None spoke, for a little, when the singing ceased. Presently, out of the corner where the home-heart sits, this comment came:

"I would rather believe that He knows all about my way and weariness *now*. I want to feel that JESUS is not one afar off, to come and to bless in some happy future, but a companion for every day, a friend in every need, a very present help in time of trouble."

"And you do not like the song then?" another asked.

"It is very sweet," said the home-heart, softly; "very sweet, and I *do* like it. It is only that I question its sentiment, or perhaps I should say its philosophy."

"But is CHRIST always so near to you? Does He never seem far off, and do you never feel that the way is dreary and the feet tired without His knowing?"

"Oh, yes!" and she sighed as she made reply. "We have doubts, all of us. We doubt the most when we are most tried and most heart-sick. But doubt and darkness are temporary. It would be folly long to give up faith. And when I sing I like best to sing of the Comforter who came when CHRIST ascended to the Father—the very Spirit of CHRIST dwelling with and abiding in us."

"But there may be songs of comfort," said the singer's voice; "even DAVID sang songs in the night. I have a fancy that the surest way out of the dark is by a path of song. The way *is* dreary, now, to some of us. It seems o me that many must find it so all along. Perhaps they have too little faith in a present CHRIST; but if they can hold on surely to their faith in a CHRIST to come, even that will bless them and make them glad. That which we long for, hope for and pray for, will surely come."

THE STILL, SMALL VOICE.

SERENE and tender shine the smiles
    Of God upon my soul to-night ;
His loving care my doubt beguiles ;
    His presence bringeth light.

The world of discord dies away ;
    I hear no more its deaf'ning din ;
And ghost-like through the evening gray
    Steal out the shapes of sin.

A holy hush is on the air ;
    A holy peace possesses me :
My very being is a prayer,
    To pray is but to be !

Did God but speak as long ago
    He spoke to prophets face to face,
I should His loving language know
    Within this holy place !

And does He not in present time
    So speak to men as once He spoke?
With awful syllables sublime
    He Sinai's silence broke ;

And not again in thunder tone
    May men His awful speaking hear,
But all the ages men have known
    His " still, small voice" anear.

So men have listened, hushed and still,
As list we now, my soul and I,
Have caught, as now we catch, the thrill
Of God's own whisper nigh !

THE HOMESICK.

THE Germans have added another beatitude to those
uttered by our SAVIOUR on the Mount—"Blessed are the
homesick, for they shall see home." There is a quaint
tenderness in it. How broad its original meaning may
have been, we can not say ; but it seems wide enough to
cover half of human kind.

There are so many homesick souls! homesick amid
wealth, and beauty, and friends—homesick in poverty
and loneliness—crying out of their discontent for the
comfort and peace of home! They hunger ; and at
home there is enough. They thirst; and at home the
pure streams of gladness flow on and on forever. Alas
for these many who are ever away from home!

Will they all reach there at last? "Blessed are they
that do hunger and thirst after righteousness, for they
shall be filled." Ah ! there is fullness at home. "Blessed are they that mourn, for they shall be comforted. "
Ah ! there is comfort, even, at home. "Blessed are the
pure in heart, for they shall see GOD !" Blessedest bless-

ing of all, GOD lives henceforth at home! "I go to pre-
pare a place for you," said the dear Brother of us all;
and He spoke then to the homesick. The place He
prepared is HOME.

It is singular that CHRIST uttered so many benedictions
upon those who want. Blessed are the hungry, blessed
are the poor, blessed are the sad—blessed, blessed, blessed, every needy soul. And so, finally, just as an out-
come of all CHRIST said, blessed are the homesick, for
they want, and must want until they see home. And
what is it they want? Love, and content, and rest.
Home means this, and more—so much more! Even as
we know how to give good gifts unto our children, so
does our Father in Heaven know how to give unto us.
Giving so freely here, what must He not give there!
Remembered so abundantly afar off, what will He not
do for us when we wander home at last!

We are journeying there, some of us, through devious
paths. Ah! if we should forget the way, and that long
night should come on in which no light can shine, and
the morning should find us wanderers yet, homeless and
homesick henceforth and forever! Blessed are the homesick, if they walk trustingly, faithfully and prayerfully on
toward the city of GOD, for to such as walk by faith the
way is sure, and they *shall* see home!

OUR BETHESDA.

In a certain sense we are invalids, all our lives long. We have in us some conscious sickness that must be cured. And we lie in expectant waiting by some Bethesda, as did those invalids of old, waiting for the angel to come and stir the waters that we may be healed.

Is not our whole life often a weary waiting for the healing? Do we not fail, frequently, to recognize God's angel when he comes in such kindly ministry? Are not the waters troubled, even while we gaze on rhem, yet without our perceiving? Weak and blind, and half despairing, do we not turn away sometimes even from the angel's very presence, and cry out in our bitterness against what has come to us and what we have missed?

If all mankind could be made whole in just the manner they wish, what a working of wonders we should see! But that can never be. The healing we most desire comes to us often by ways we do not prefigure, and to our dull consciousness it is no healing at all. Lying by our Bethesda, if we see the waters troubled it is for another, and we wait on, not taking what is really meant for us. If our healing should come through love and warm sympathy, we long for it, and then turn it aside when offered. If faith would work the perfect cure we need, we spurn it when it comes knocking gently at our heart's door, and in unbelief and doubting wait on. If sweet charity to all in thought and deed would make us well, we cast it aside for that which is embittering and unkind, and watch for the angel's coming with a light in our eyes that would make of every angel almost a demon.

Is it strange, then, that we go unhealed? Is it strange that at every pool of gladness and joy-giving we lie in waiting all the years long? To be made whole is the supreme want. Humanly speaking each lacks something. That lack must be supplied, and only our dear LORD's angelic ministers can supply it. May they trouble the waters for us all, and speedily! Divinely speaking, each lacks everything, lacking a childlike trust in and love for that most loving of all GOD's ministers, His only begotten Son. And may He trouble the waters of our soul until the healing is perfect, and then grant us that peace which passeth understanding!

THE man who walks the street recognizing the excellences of other men and honoring them, will find his fellows conceding and esteeming his own virtues. He who gives helping sympathy, abundantly and warmly, to the suffering and sad, will himself have help and sympathy, abundant and warm, when he suffers and is sad.

THY ROD AND STAFF.

PERPLEXED I walk my weary way,
In doubt and darkness, day by day ;
I see no earthly light to cheer,
I find no earthly comfort near ;
But weak and fainting though I be,
" Thy rod and staff they comfort me !"

I seek some friendly arm to aid,
The help I need is long delayed :
I look for love to hold me fast,
No human love will always last:
But though all earthly helpers flee,
" Thy rod and staff they comfort me !"

My burdens yet more heavy grow,
As on the weary way I go ;
And faint and hungered, weak and worn,
The while for losses great I mourn,
In longing sore I turn to Thee,—
" Thy rod and staff they comfort me !"

Beneath Thy smitings oft I shrink ;
Thy bitter cups I would not drink ;
I turn aside some path to find,
That through a better land shall wind,
Yet looking back, Thy face I see,—
" Thy rod and staff they comfort me !"

And so I walk the weary way
Where'er Thou leadest, day by day ;

Though smitten sore, I'll onward press
Till I the Promised Land possess ;
For faint and burdened though I be,
" Thy rod and staff they comfort me !"

GRACES OF HOLINESS.

A VISITOR is with us to-night and we ask about former acquaintances—has this one changed?—has that one grown old ?   To the latter question, in one instance, our friend replies,—"She has too much spiritual beauty in her face ever to grow old."

We remember her face well, and RUTH says, " Yes, hers was the beauty of holiness, if we ever see it on earth ; " and this application of a phrase rarely so applied does not seem wrong.

Character does show itself in the countenance ; the inward grace of a real religious life will shine out, in a way we may not quite describe.   When faith, and love, and patience all unite to beautify a Christian soul, is it strange that the face takes on a rare sort of beauty which years can not dim?

The light in some faces is like a benediction of peace. It is at once a blessing and a declaration.   Nothing but the purest piety makes it to glow there : it blesses you as by a holy influenc ; it tells of devotion never failing, of untroubled faith, of perfect hope, of undivided love.

STEPHEN's face wore it ; they must have seen it who saw
the beloved JOHN. It has beautified the features of every
saint on earth ; it is one of the beauties of every saint
in heaven.

Such a beauty of holiness comes not by the seeking of
it. Like all true graces, it is an unconscious possession,
won not for itself. But it is always a proof of possibilities in the Christirn life. It is ever a witness for higher
Christian character. It is a living testimony that care
and tribulation and disappointment need not mar the
soul's peace. For you shall find, search where you will,
that this beauty spiritual lies with those who have suffered, and borne burdens, and been driven, so, near to
GOD. Holiness follows and must follow, overcoming.
The beauties of it, the outward manifestations of it, are
results of unselfish upgiving, of complete trust, of never
doubting or rarely doubting love.

HUMAN DESIRES.

WHAT are they ? What ought they to be ?

We may not doff our humanity untit death comes, but
we may discipline it, purify it by such disciplining, make
it a worthier thing. We may, with GOD's help.

But will we ? To do it, much of our desire must
undergo change. Whereas we now long for that which
wonld in no wise ennoble, we must long for that which

will inevitably do that.　　Whereas self now prompts every ambition, self must be ruled over until ambitions spring from another source—the love of GOD within us.

Yet can we put thought in a strait jacket?　Can we persistently check impure desires, unholy aspirations, and help on the work of improving our moral nature?　It seems a hard task ; it is a hard task.　　Appetite is strong ; passion is often master.　Prayer at times is apparently of no avail.　Everything that is evil in our hearts fights tenaciously for full possession, and often full possession is granted.　　Then we go down—down in our own con- sciousness.　We lose self-respect ; we feel less and less zeal in behalf of the true and pure.

We all know what such experiences are.　Is there any- thing sadder? And where is the remedy?　We can answer well enough in our theory; it sometimes proves more difficult in actual fact.　The difficulty arises mainly, we think, from just a lack of self-discipline.　Even effica- cious prayer is rendered inefficient, at times, through this common lack.　It is useless to pray for purity of thought and desire, and still let the imagination continually run riot over forbidden fields with never an effort at checking it.　It is idle to hope for answers to such prayer, when back of it there is no earnest resolve to be self-helpful, and to strive continually for better things.　Human de- sires can be purified only through human discipline, and much of this can be carried on by self alone.

AS A PRODIGAL.

It is evening, Lord. I have had my day
  Out in the wilderness, far from Thee,
Bright was the morn when I went away,
  Happy my visions of joy to be.

In the hot high noon I was weak and faint,
  Worn with rioting, heartsick, sore ;
Never I murmured or made complaint ;
  Onward I crept to the sands before.

What if they blistered my naked feet ?
  Better to suffer than turn back now.
What if I 'd nothing but husks to eat ?
  Pride may starve, but it will not bow.

And what if with swine I could only mate
  Out in the barren and dusty field?
What if I pined for my lost estate ?
  Pride may die, but it will not yield.

Pride may die. And my pride is dead—
  Dead, and buried where sleep the swine.
" I will return !" to myself I said :
  " Home !—my Father's, that once was mine !"

It is evening, Lord, and I come to Thee,
  Weak and hungry, and faint and sore.
Look in Thy pitiful love on me ;
  Spurn me not from Thine open door !

It is evening, now, and my day is spent ;
  Little of life may be mine, beside—
Only a season of glad content,
  All my hungering satisfied !

PAIN'S MINISTRIES.

PAIN is our birthright.   It comes to us, as certainly as the days come.

Can anything sent of GOD be without its blessing ? Is there no sweet ministry even in pain ? Do we simply suffer and be still ? Or do we suffer and grow strong ?

Suffer we must.   Either our health fails, or friends die or plans miscarry, or love proves false, or hope cheats, and whichever it be, there will ensue suffering.   There is nothing so common as pain.   There is no experience so inevitable.

What the ministry of pain may be, will depend wholly upon how we bear suffering—upon the spirit in which we suffer.   If pain is rebelled against, as an unjust visitation from GOD—if we say constantly to ourselves the while we suffer, "GOD is unkind and cruel"—the ministry will be a ministry of hurting.   And to how many souls it is all this, and only this !   How many charge hard things against their Maker, and go on through the years gathering no s eet fruit from the tree of bitter blossoms !

Blessed indeed are those who can give thanks even amid their suffering—who can smile in GOD's face while the hurt cuts like a knife—who can feel that something is to come of the hurt besides scars and soreness. Blessed with a rare blessedness are they who sing softly to themselves though the heart be sad—who sing because they *know* that from this darkness of sorrow shall come a light glad and beautiful, and, better than all, healing. The Angel of Pain is kinder to us than we think. Would that all could say with SAXE HOLM :

> Angel of Pain, I think thy face
> Will be, in all the heavenly place,
> The sweetest face that I shall see,
> And swiftest face to shine on me.
> All other angels faint and tire ;
> Joy wearies, and forsakes desire ;
> Hope falters, face to face with Fate,
> And dies because it can not wait ;
> And love cuts short each loving day,
> Because fond hearts can not obey
> That subtlest law which measures bliss
> By what it is content to miss.
> But thou, O loving, faithful Pain—-
> Hated, reproached rejected, slain—
> Dost only closer cling and bless
> In sweeter, stronger steadfastness.
> Dear, patient angel, to thine own
> Thou comest, and art never known
> Till late, in some lone twilight place
> The light of thy transfigured face
> Sudden shines out, and, speechless, they
> Know they have walked with Christ all day.

LIFE is one continuous round of beginnings and endings. And yet how few days are finished! How few evenings see the morning's beginning properly ended!

We misjudge our deed greatly when we say it is done. Done in its narrowest sense it surely is ; done in its broadest meaning it as surely is not. A finished thing is put away. Do we in fact put any doing entirely out of our life? Would that we could, sometimes ! We should be better, so.

Herein lies much of the bitterness of being—that the weak things done, or the things weakly done, never can be wholly laid aside. We hold on to them despite ourselves. They are a part of us, because a part of our experience. The experience is the man, in very deed. You cannot put your self apart from your self's acts and say "I am better than these." Self's acts are a vital part of self.

Our beginnings, therefore, have only apparent endings. Be they for good or ill, they run on through the gathering years, and end never. It is well to think of this, whenever the day fades into twilight—to realize that every attempt made during its brief hours tells ever after, in a greater or less degree, upon our life; that every accomplishment, seemingly completed, goes on in influence through the after-days, and dims not into utter fading. The work of this hour over-laps the labor of the next, and the two a.e bound together by invisible cords. So the life here and the life hereafter interblend ; the doing of the mortal will mold the being of the immortal beyond all possibility of changing.

THE OTHER SIDE.

WE go our ways in life too much alone ;
　We hold ourselves too far from all our kind.
Too often are we deaf to sigh and moan ;
　Too often to the weak and helpless blind ;
Too often, where distress and want abide,
We turn and pass upon the other side !

The other side is trodden smooth and worn
　By foot-steps passing idly all the day ;
Where lie the bruised ones, the faint and torn,
　Is seldom more than an untrodden way ;
Our selfish hearts are for our feet the guide,
They lead us by upon the other side !

It should be ours the oil and wine to pour
　Into the bleeding wounds of stricken ones ;
To take the smitten, and the sick and sore,
　And bear them where a stream of blessing runs ;
Instead, we look about—the way is wide—
And so we pass upon the other side !

O, friends and brothers, hast'ning down the years,
    Humanity is calling each and all
In tender accents, born of pain and tears!
    I pray you listen to the thrilling call!
You cannot, in your selfishness and pride,
Pass *guiltless* by upon the other side!

THE SIN OF INDIFFERENCE.

IT is an all-prevailing sin. Men everywhere seem reck-less of the future, indifferent as to what their eternity may be. They live wholly in and for the present, and care for naught else. It is as though they said, "This life only is mine and I must make the most of it. To-day is and To-morrow may not be." Indeed, do they not say it in their hearts?

And yet each morning and evening should make men thoughtful of a coming time. Each hour is indeed a fact, but more than a fact. It is a suggestion—a hint of future ages. The hour may mean much, may comprise much, but that which it hints of means infinitely more, comprises so much more that no one can comprehend it. Eternity is a word which the dictionary of life does not define; we can not satisfy ourselves of its marvelous scope.

But because we do not understand, are we excusable for complete indifference? Because GOD is a mystery in-

penetrable, may we ignore His existence? We do, though.
We breathe with no thought of Him who gives us the
power to breathe. We enjoy all the sweet and beautiful
with no regard for Him who enables us to enjoy. We
take life and all its attendant circumstances as a matter-
of-course, worth little or much, as fate may ordain.

GOD has a right to more thoughtful regard on the part
of His creatures. It becomes us to shake off this sin of
indifference and concede the Creator His due.

FOOLISH DARING.

IT is better, after all, to be a coward in some things.
And why?

Because to be brave in the face of certain dangers—
dangers of certain kinds—is to run foolish risks uncalled
for, and from the very nature of things bound to result
in some degree of evil.

There are young men in the gutters to-day who were
first brave, as all young men are, and then weak, as so
many young men are sure to be. Their bravery worked
their ruin. They insisted on proving dangers that they
might have let alone in all honor—that they might even
have fled from without disgrace.

So there are professed Christians to-day in the Slough
of Despond because they foolishly dared to brave dangers

to their faith which they might readily enough have shun-
ned. They could dally with vague speculations, they
thought, without any harm, and so dallying they passed
under the cloud.

Society, on all sides, is full of temptations that invite
daring. They beckon every man and woman of us onward ; and the mistaken notion that it is brave to test
them impels thousands to destruction. A man may
walk a rope over the very brink of Niagara, and come off
safely, but he is infinitely safer if he make no such
attempt. He only who keeps away from danger knows
what perfect security is.

If we hold life as of no worth, and the future as not to
be regarded, why then let us test every danger that may
perchance wreck us. But who so thinks? Talk lightly
as we may of what living amounts to, it does amount to
so much for each and every one of us that we would not
willingly give it up. How shall we best keep it? By
clinging to the safe side. If any life is worth aught, the
best life is worth the most, and the best life is the safe
life. There is no truer logic. In the face of it, then,
can we go on testing dangers that bring no good in the
proving?

OUR GUIDES.

In a pillar of cloud by day, O God,
    And a pillar of fire by night,
Thy presence did guide on the way they trod
    Thy people of old in flight ;
And the wilderness way that we walk to-day
    More dreary and dark would seem,
If through the deep night, or the twilight gray,
    Thy presence should never gleam.

I am glad that they waited in days of old,
    With a promise of better things ;
For my heart it is stirred when the tale is told
    By the hope and the cheer it brings.
I am glad that they journeyed those forty years
    In trouble, and doubt, and pain,
For the gloom of my wilderness disappears
    At thought of their final gain.

We may never quite perfectly understand
    Why the wilderness waits for each,
Yet we know that the beautiful Promised Land
    Is beyond it—without our reach ;
But whatever the burdens we have to bear,
    Or however we shrink and faint,
We shall carry ourselves and our burdens there,
    If a prayer is our sole complaint !

Had they only looked down in the olden time,
    As they journeyed with falt'ring tread,

They would never have known of the guides sublime
    That forever their foot-steps led ;
And I pray though we walk in a faithless way,
    Though we seldom look up for light,
We may never lose thought of the cloud by day,
    Or the pillar of fire by night !

HUMAN AFFECTION.

THE preacher said sweetly comforting things this morning, in regard to love as an influence in religious life. In certain ages, and even to-day in certain places, men have sought to divorce religion and affection—have endeavored to put the two far apart. They have acted upon the mistaken theory that piety means asceticism— that to grow in spiritual grace they must become dead to everything tenderly and lovingly human—must hold themselves separate from their kind and acknowledge no brotherhood with their fellows. So they have become hermits, and have lived the life of the recluse.

But all this is wrong. The best men of the Bible were live men,—men who cherished sweet affections and hesitated not to declare them. The most lion-hearted in their dealings with sin were the most lamb-like in loving, —tender and true. In the common things of the world, so called, those characters are of most worth in which there abounds fullness of affection—in which there throbs

a large, live heart. And so in Christian life, they serve
GOD best whose out-reaching sympathies compel wide
service for humanity, —who know all men in a common
brotherhood, and are moved by human needs to noble
doing.

Sometimes it happens that the husband or the wife
hesitates to urge his or her companion on to a Christian
walk, fearing separation must come between. But how
can separation come, when love to GOD only increases
love to all His creatures? GOD is not jealous in this
matter. Is it a sign, because He took away your child,
that He hated the child?—that He was jealous of the
love your child drew forth? Not so. He only loved the
little one more than you loved it—loved it so well that
He would spare it all possibility of sin and pain. GOD's
very nature is love; and what He implanted in the heart
of humanity He will not rebuke.

There are Christian homes wherein love seems restrain-
ed, in which there is little of manifest affection. Is
such a state of things in full accord with our SAVIOUR's
Gospel? Did CHRIST restore LAZARUS from the dead
simply as an exhibition of His miraculous power? We
think not. We prefer to believe the restoration was a
tribute to the rare love of those weeping sisters. Human
affection is a blessed influence in this religion of ours;
the influence broadens and deepens in proportion as
this affection is broad and deep, and unrestrained. Say
you that we must not worship what GOD has given us?
Love is not worship; it never need be. It is another
thing in character, in very essence. Love indeed, is a

Christian duty, and so is worship—of a certain kind : in so far they are kin. Unless religion warms our heart toward wife and child—toward all human kind—it is scarcely to be trusted.

MEASURING CHARACTER.

It is not so much what we are, as what we ought to be, that should be regarded. We have no right to look at our strict morality, our outward appearance, the name we have in community, and because of these pronounce ourselves very good, very praiseworthy. We may be negatively good—good because not bad—good because no strong temptation has overcome us and swept us away into sin—good because from our temperament we can hardly be guilty of overt crime.

Positive goodness is another thing. We may fall far short of it and yet be quite respectable. It is by the standard of that alone that we should be judged, or by the standard of our possibility to attain unto it. One man's character is very good for him, when it would be very *mediocre* for his next neighbor, who is capable of excellence far exceeding any he can ever reach. The neighbor may have a character really commendable, as an average, but not by any means up to what it should be, considering his possibilities of progression.

For character is not simply neighborhood standing.
There are men in good repute with their fellows who
have not much character to boast of. They are negatives.
They lack an essential something to make them strong
and valuable. They are never workers in reform, leaders
in good works, earnest, efficient, zealous. What they
do is creditable, but they do so little thatthe credit side of
the sheet shows poorly enough against the debit of what
they might do and should do.

We are responsible for omissions, as for commissions.
Given the power to do, and failing to do, we are mani-
festly culpable. Our SAVIOUR in His parable of the Ten
Talents emphasizes this great truth, and so earnestly that
there is no mistaking. That which we have will not long
be ours unless we put it to use.

THY PEACE.

FATHER, O Father ! the sunlight is vanished,
   Swiftly the evening descends on my soul ;
Comfort and cheer from my bosom are banished,   .
   Billows of bitterness over me roll,
Hearken again to my anguished petition,—
   Give me Thy peace, in the midst of my pain !
Grant me the grace of a patient submission,
   Bring me new hope as my courage shall wane.

Father ! O Father ! forlorn I am groping
   On in a way that is shrouded in gloom ;
Faint is my purpose, and weary my hoping,—
   Is there no rest till I come to the tomb ?
Answer the cry of my soul in its pleading,—
   Give me Thy peace that I stronger may be,
Patient to follow the path of Thy leading,—
   Patient to grope until light I can see !

Father ! O Father ! I'm worn with the faring ; ·
   Hunger and thirst with the darkness increase,
Hunger and thirst for the boon of Thy caring,
   Hunger and thirst for the gift of Thy peace.
Listen again to the cry of my spirit, —
   Born of its need and its bitter unrest;
Bow down the ear of Thy mercy and hear it,
   Speak to the waves in my storm-troubled breast !

Father, O Father ! the night season thickens,
   Darker the way as I painfully grope ;
Faith of its watchfulness wearies and sickens,
   Faints to despairing the patience of hope.
Hear the deep cry of my agony, thrilling
   Through the long night of my wandering here,
Then shall Thy peace, every passion wave stilling,
   Fill me and thrill me till daylight appear !

GOD'S FATHERHOOD.

As the twilight comes on, the domesticity of our nature makes itself most felt. We are not now ourselves alone; we are part of that sweet family circle in which we sit—part of it in love and tenderness and mutual sympathy. Meditation is not so much loneliness of thought, as thought realizing close association with others.

In a certain sense we are never so near our friends as when we sit with them separated only by silence—when our hearts go out to meet theirs in that silent communion which forbids all speech. Then indeed are we as children of one parent, and GOD is our FATHER, in a fatherhood so near and helpful, so complete and satisfying, that its recognition lifts us gladly heavenward.

And sitting here in the shadow, with our Home tokens all about us, it is comforting to whisper softly those sweet words of the Psalmist—"Like as a father pitieth his children, so the LORD pitieth them that fear Him." The human side of GOD's love speaks out in this. For is it irreverent to think of GOD as loving with somewhat of human affection? Can we not gain some little idea of Divine Fatherhood from a comprehension of fatherhood not divine?

But GOD's Fatherhood is infinite in its many-sidedness, and on that account we fail to measure it. The preacher ·

well said, this morning, "I will accept no man's idea of
the whole heavens, which simply takes in the little thereof that he can see from his narrow chamber window."
The infinite Fatherhood is more than it seems to us.
The relations of one child to the parent, are not the
relations of all the children. Temperaments differ, dispositions are diverse. To you, GOD may seem to be
Justice, and you may fear Him, knowing your sins. To
another He may stand as Holiness, and impurity may
shrink from His presence. To yet another, He may
appear only Love, and trusting faith may lose itself in
His great affection.

The Fatherhood of GOD includes all these, and even
more. Yet, while we must all realize, in some degree,
GOD's Justice, His Holiness, we need not to keep these
ever foremost in our mind when thinking of Him. The
justice and the holiness need not shut us out from that
over-brooding love which watches ever for our coming.
GOD's love and pity are as broad as humanity—aye, broader than that—as broad as the great Divine Nature in
which they live evermore, from which they freely flow.

THE world-life is a great web, and GOD, the weaver, is
working it out. If we look at only a small part of it,
there seems no design, nothing but a fragment. But if
our eye can take in the entire web, the design is at once
apparent.

HUNGERING AND THIRSTING.

HUNGER and thirst are the strongest human besetments. Have you ever hungered almost to the point of starving, or been so a-thirst that the brain reeled and all your being seemed on fire? Then you can conceive, in a measure, what a depth of meaning is hidden in that phrase, "Hunger and thirst after righteousness."

When we are sorely an hungered, the supreme want is food; when we thirst to unquenchable inward burning, the supreme want is drink. Just so when we hunger and thirst spiritually, will the supreme want be righteousness,—a renewing of the life within, a purifying of the soul, a cleansing from every and all sin. How seldom we so hunger and thirst. We have appetites for everything else but this. Debasing pleasures rarely cloy us; we partake of them without loss of relish. Secret sins we roll under our tongues with never abating enjoyment; they never weary us as daily food.

Then why may there not be this other hungering? It brings its own blessing. The promise is that "they shall be filled" who do thus hunger and thirst aright.

Filled! It is a sweet word, with no limitations such as rob many another of complete meaning. It is the same as satisfied. And who was ever satisfied in any other way than this? No cloying of common appetite

4

ever yet fully satisfied a man. Cloyed of one thing—
one pleasure—one gratification—he invariably turns to
something else with an irresistible longing.

God's righteousness so fills us there is nothing want-
ed beside. But it never fills unless longed for, hungered
for, thirsted for. Unless it be the supreme want of the
soul it never makes the soul inexpressibly glad. Is there
something desired after more than this? Then we shall
never be filled. Is there something we are willing to
sacrifice more for than this? Then sacrifice will never
bring its final and fruitful reward. Completely blessed
alone are they who do hunger and thirst after righteousness.

A HEART SONG.

Singer, softly sing to-night—
  "God is good and just;"
And in darkness or in light
  In Him put your trust;
Sing the song till earthly sight
  Fades in "dust to dus ."

Singer, softly sing and low—
  "God is love alway;"
Let the heart in tender flow
  Melt the words you say;
Then shall you God's loving know
  Sweetly day by day.

DIVINE ORDERING.

SITTING here in the twilight—in the sweet uncertainty that seems to brood over all things—when that which to-day is fades into dreamfulness, and that which is to be on the morrow is yet unborn—it is blessed to feel that the world is not ruled by chance, and that Divine orderings link the days together. Conceive the thought of a universe without GOD, and you at once fall into doubt of all things. There is no certainty. On nothing can you rely. Would we care to live longer under such circumstances?

Our every surrounding testifies to an Omniscient Hand and its working. There is order in the minutest particulars, and the ordering is so perfect, so wonderfully wise, that we feel it must be divine. GOD works always with the most rigid exactness as to detail. A pleasant writer tells of a Texas gentleman who had the misfortune to be an unbeliever. One day he was walking in the woods, reading the writings of PLATO. Coming to where that great writer uses the phrase, "GOD geometrizing," he thought to himself, "If I could only see plan and order in GOD's works, I could be a believer."

Just then he saw a little "Texas Star" at his feet, and picking it up, he began thoughtlessly to count its petals. There were five. Counting the stamens, he found there were five of these. Counting the divisions at the base of the flower, he found five of these. Then he set about multiplying these three fives, to see how many chances there were of a flower being brought into existence with-out the aid of mind, and having these three fives. The chances against it were one hundred and twenty-five to one.

He thought that was very strange. He examined another flower and found it the same. He multiplied one hundred and twenty-five by itself to see how many chances there were against there being two flowers, each having these exact relations of numbers. He found the chances against it were thirteen thousand six hundred and twenty-five to one. But all around him were multi-tudes of these little flowers; they had been growing and blooming there for years. He thought this showed the order of intelligence, and that the mind that ordained it was God. And so he shut up his book, and picked up the little flower, and kissed it, and exclaimed, "Bloom on, little flowers; sing on, little birds; you have a God, and I have a God; the God that made these little flowers made me!"

THE SERVICE OF WAITING.

O LORD, Thy servants all about I see,
   In faithful service working as they may ;
I stand here idle, doing nought for Thee,
   And poor, unprofitable, seems my day.
Will fruitful labor bless me, even late ?
" They also serve who only stand and wait. "

This is Thy answer.   Give me patience, then,
   And help me all the while I waiting stand
To know that every service had of men
   Is by Thy providential wisdom planned.
So shall I feel, though waiting may be sore,
That Thy great goodness hath reward in store !

And so may I of patient service give
   That my own being shall more fruitful grow,
And I shall in my waiting learn to live
   A better life than haply I might know
If, in the press of busy doing, I
Should miss, at times, the Master standing by !

O Lord, I thank Thee I may serve at all !
   What need hast Thou of service such as mine ?
I thank Thee that Thy benedictions fall
   Alike upon all laborers of Thine !
I thank Thee for this comfort sweet and great—
" They also serve who only stand and wait ! "

"For me to live is CHRIST."

PAUL said that, years and years ago. The preacher took up the words this morning, and turned them over and over until their fullness stood out strong and clear to our apprehension.

Going back to the initial point,—what is life, any way, to you and to me? For *us* to live is—what? Gain, pleasure, personal ease, ambition gratified, tastes indulged, passion pandered to (GOD forbid!), in a word, *self!* Alas! too often these, or a portion thereof.

PAUL meets us with an exemplary declaration which we should ever keep in mind—a declaration which only persistent self-discipline could have enabled him truthfully to make—and in the face of it we must acknowledge how far short of real nobility our life comes. Christianity is a daily being and doing; not an impulse, not the gratification of selfish desires, or the occasional following out of purer promptings, but the actual living of CHRIST. Which is to say that the underlying motive of being and doing must come from CHRIST—that we must allow Him to fill us, and inspire us, and uplift us.

PAUL came to what he could truly say through much of struggle and conquering. In the natural condition of things for man to live is *not* CHRIST, but man's self.

PAUL had grown out of this condition,—had gone beyond it, as we must go beyond it if ever we do—over the ruins of much prized selfish things. Have we the heart for such discipline? It must come in the street, at the desk, in the daily duty, in the home. Our hours of labor must be full of it; in the restful seasons into which we now and then retire it must not be forgotten.

So the real CHRIST-life is more than a passing enjoyment. It is a perpetual self-crucifixon. Is there then no pleasure in it? PAUL testified how much it was to him, albeit he had sorer trials than often visit us. Since his time thousands have taken up the testimony and emphasized it, in every clime. Men count pleasure differently. But the highest pleasure satisfies most and longest, and the CHRIST-life means satisfaction longer and more complete than that arising from any other source. Does it not? Even with our little taste of it can we not give affirmative answer?

As we give the best we have, we get the best we can have. The most unmistakable illustration of this general truth is in its highest application. The rarest donation any one can offer is himself in the completeness of his nature and and possession, to CHRIST; and when this is done he receives in return the choicest blessing he can appropriate, the filling of himself with GOD.

"ABIDE with us!" was the prayer of our SAVIOUR'S disciples on a memorable occasion.

It was toward evening; the night was coming on; their hearts had burned within them while talking together by the way, and it would be more pleasant with such a guest after the day's ending.

It is toward evening with us all, perhaps. Sooner than we think may the night fall upon us, dark and dreary. If not the night of death, then such a night as settles down only too often upon every life, when it is thick darkness all about. And we need to pray earnestly for CHRIST to abide with us.

For when there is no comfort, shall we not need the Comforter? When all that is bright and gladsome seems shut out, shall we not long intensely for the brightness and sweet cheer that might be ours? Such times will come; they come to each one of us. They are inevitable. Nights must complement the days, in the common order of nature. Whosoever is sensitive to pleasure is surely sensitive to pain, and the one will come as truly as will the other. "Much must be borne that it is hard to bear," said one once, and each heart will echo the truth of that saying.

But thank GOD that for the Christian there is never a night without its stars! Since the early morning, so many years agone, when that star rose in the East, all who have sincerely acknowledged the Babe of Bethlehem as a would's Reedemer, have seen some ray in every deepening gloom, and have felt rare comfort when life were else quite comfortless.

We may not hope that CHRIST will walk with us as He walked with the disciples of old, yet may His presence be to us as sure a reality as it was to them. Aye, even more. The incarnate GOD was not so much a fact to those who listened to His preaching, and enjoyed His companionship, as He is now to us. He has been more to us than He ever was to them, because in a certain sense we have all that He has been to mankind through these eighteen hundred years.

"Abide with us!" Breathe forth your prayer, O sin-sick heart! Your evening is not far off at the most. Even if CHRIST fail at once to answer, He will return presently, and you shall know exceeding joy.

THE PURE IN HEART.

"THE pure in heart are blest," He said,
    Who on the mountain taught,
Ere on the Cross His blood He shed,
    And our salvation wrought.
O blessed words that blessing gave !
    I hear their echo yet,
And all their promised good I crave
    Who evil would forget.

Yet can the blessing e'er be mine?
   I question, full of fear;
I am so far from all divine,
   To all of earth so near;
There crowds into my life so much
   To blacken and degrade ;
Sin jostles with so rude a touch
   Each holy help and aid !

An answer comes with comfort sweet
   My troubling fear to still,
" All promises fulfillment meet
   For those who do My will ;
That which you long for, pray for, seek,
   Is somehow now possest,
The words are certain that I speak—
   The pure in heart *are* blest !"

THE ENDLESS DAY.

SCRIPTURE silence is never more marked thaa in regard
to our future state.   There is little in the way of definite
information touching our hereafter, to be found in the
Bible.   Much is said in a figurative sense, and this is
indeed a solace.   Just how much of it is figurative, who
can tell?

Of the few explicit statements made about heaven,
theie is nothing more beautiful and satisfying than this,
—" There shall be no night there." There is so much

night here! So often the shadows come down over us,
snd shut us in like a shroud! So somber grow the evenings, and so few the stars! It must be a radiant country,
where it is daylight forever and forever.

"Neither sorrow nor crying." Nights bring sorrow,
frequently. Sorrow makes night, whenever sorrow comes.
Many are the mornings bright and golden which
have turned into darkest night ere the noon-tide. Thank
GOD, all ye sorrowing ones, that there is coming a morning which shall be dimmed by never a cloud! which
shall never fade into evening! which shall shine on
through the ages of eternity unchanged, unchanging.

There may be no gates of pearl,—no streets of gold,
—all this may be figurative as regards that heaven most
of us hope for, but let us still believe that in heaven
there will be an endless day. Ye image-breakers who
would spoil our prettiest pictures of the beyond by de-
claring all revelation only figurative, spare us this as literal. Literal our inner natures declare it. All who
sorrow and weep would go wild with despair in their
sorrowing and weeping, did they not have faith in an
actual freedom from grief and tears by-and-by. And that
which is so fully borne in upon our deeper natures is
generally true. By some subtle prescience we see somewhat of the hidden in a manner we cannot explain. So
let us comfort ourselves in the belief which is tender and
comforting as words of peace can be,—"There shall be
no night there!"

THE ANGEL OF HEALING.

O, ALL of our life we lie beside
　Some pool of Bethesda here,
And wait for the angel its waves to stir
　With waiting that has no cheer;
For never the angel appears to us,
　The waters are always still,
The healing we ever impa ient wait
　Comes never with healing thrill.

And so by the waters we sit and sigh,
　Our being a sad complaint,
The hope of the morning growing dim,
　The heart of our manhood faint;
But miracles never are wrought, to-day,
　And though we are faint and sore,
T 'is idle to linger the pool beside,
　The waters will stir no more!

The angels of heaven are all abroad,
　We meet them in busy marts,
They enter the plainest of humble homes,
　They visit the poorest hearts;
But silent they come, and silent work,
　And all unheeding are we,
Tho' needed the gift that they bring to us,
　Whatever the gift may be.

Not always the want we feel the most
　Should fully for us be met;

God knoweth our need—our need of needs—
   And He will never forget!
Then why should we sit in complaining mood,
   In hope that is half a fear?
Unseen, but ready to minister,
   The Angel of GOD is near!

THE DEEPER REST.

"I TRUSTED too little, and reasoned too much," said
one, referring to a great mistake in life.   "I should have
reasoned less, and trusted more."

Many of our mistakes grow out of this lack of trust.
It is human to rely on reason, on self.   It is hard to
wait patiently on the LORD.   Is a way clearly pointed out
to us? we hesitate to walk therein until we see reasons
for the going.   Is a difficult thing plainly set before us
for accomplishing? we falter, and cast about for convin-
cing proof that do it we must.

And how often we argue with GOD! How often we
utterly let go of Trust, and hold only to Reason! Yet
it is harder to dispute with Providence, than to accept
every leading unhesitatingly.   Harder, if so be to trust
has become a little natural to us.   Harder, any how, as a
matter of fact.   Where GOD leads, it is easy going, if
one go believing.   When reason goes against GOD, the
way is steep at the end, if smooth and pleasant first,—

steep and rough, and it comes out among brambles that vex and make sore.

Is absolute trust possible? To those who really rest in CHRIST, yes. Now and then some one speaks of a deeper rest than the many know, and such testimony is gratifying. What does this deeper rest signify? RUTH was reading in a little book entitled "The Rest of Faith," this afternoon, and here the story of such a rest was told. We have listened to the telling, orally, by another who struggled through much of doubt and questioning into perfect trust. Such trust is not attained to in an hour. It is the fruit of long-suffering in spirit and repeated cross-bearing. It is the answer to burdened prayer.

"Come unto me all ye that labor, and are heavy laden and I will give you rest." There is more here than a promise, though as a promise, the words are sweet and strong. There is an implication, inferentially a statement, that those without rest are away from CHRIST. And beyond question the implication is true. We lack the rest because we are afar off. Do we feel troubled, and distressed, and doubtful of the future? Then surely we are not near to GOD. To us, especially, is it said, "Come." Unto whom? Faith knows, even the little faith we have. Faith believes on Him, and takes to itself, in a measure, the promise He has made. Yet it is only a half faith. It will, by-and-by, doubt, and step aside for reason, until shall come the deeper rest, wherein not a doubt is harbored, no questioning put forth, but all is serenity and peace —the peace of GOD.

THE preacher's theme this morning grew out of that sad story of LOT—a story full of lessons for us all.

You know when LOT divided the land with his covetous relative, he "pitched his tent toward Sodom." Why? Because self-interest, as he believed, centered there. He did not go as a missionary; he had no hope of purifying that pool of iniquity. He went there for gain. Doubtless the Sodomites knew it, and laughed at any moral suasion he may have attempted. The result is familiar to all.

And there are many men to-day pitching their tent toward Sodom. Men of politics, who make use of unworthy means to accomplish political success; to whom party gain is greater than the dominance of principle. Men of trade, who indulge undue desires to get on, and who get on unduly—who sacrifice strict probity on the altar of mercantile success. All sorts of men, who in any form ignore right and just dealing and doing, and look first to selfish ends, last to the means which win them.

Toward Sodom! Sodom was laid in ashes, yet Sodom exists even now. In ruins centuries ago, it is still to thousands of people a delightful city of gain and all good things, wherein every desire shall be satisfied. Men go toward it as toward a Mecca. They dwell in it, amid its vice, its varied evils, and are content. And when comes the cry of "Up! Get thee out!" they pay little heed.

Toward Sodom! "Every road leads to the world's end," read an old legend. It were sad indeed, if many were to reach the world's end through Sodom ; if selfishness were to overrule all other considerations, until they should become veritable Sodomites of a later day, only to perish as miserably as perished the Sodomites of old.

DAY BY DAY.

WE should live as though doing days' works for GOD. There is no contract for long service. It is day by day, and day by day. Our master may have need for us further on ; He may not. It is not ours to question. Good and faithful service, now, is the thing asked. And to strengthen us for the day's work we should be given our daily bread. The prayer for it so brief, so simple, covers every human need. It means bread for the body and bread for the soul ; physical and spiritual nourishment. Is our prayer an earnest and honest one? Do we really crave of GOD our daily food? Or are we seeking to satisfy human cravings from some other source? "Give us this day our daily bread." How many pray thus in the truest sense, as CHRIST taught?

"ONE WITH THE LORD."

"ONE with the Lord!" Will the day of my dying
   Bring me so glad and so sweet a reward,
For all of my waiting, my sorrow and sighing,
   As that of the making me "one with the Lord?"

Here there is little of good in communion ;
   Little of sweets with my life interblend ;
I long in my loneliness e'er for the union
   Which through an eternity never shall end.

"One with the Lord!" Dare I hope for such blessing?
   Hope for a crowning so royal as this?
Shall such at the last be my certain possessing?
   Shall such be the sum of my infinite bliss?

Recompense lesser would pay me for waiting;
   Sorrow might smile for a reason less sweet ;
My heart might believe it were heav'n antedating
   To thrill with a joy not the half so complete.

Often I miss the dear face of my Saviour ;
   Often I wander away from His side ;
Between us, too often, my sinful behavior
   Creates separation despairingly wide.

There in the glow of the glory so golden,
   There in the mansion preparing for me,
Henceforth, from all wanderings ever enfolden,
   O "One with the Lord!" let me finally be !

JEPHTHAH'S DAUGHTER.

GOING out to do battle against the Ammonites, JEPH-THAH, the newly elected Captain of Israel, made a vow. It was his ambition to conquer a peace and reign long over the Israelites. Moreover, he hoped to leave his family in direct succession to the rulership. To gratify his ambitious desires, he was ready to make any sacrifice. So he "vowed a vow unto the Lord, and said, If thou shalt without fail, deliver the children of Ammon into my hands, then it shall be that whatsoever cometh forth of the doors of my house to meet me, when I return in peace from the children of Ammon, shall surely be the LORD's, and I will offer it up for a burnt-offering."

It was a rash vow, and a thoughtless one. The Lord gave him victory, and returning to Mizpeh in triumph the first person to greet him was his only daughter—his only child. Here was a shock, indeed! To what a strait had his unwise vowing brought him! In obedience to the vow made to obtain the object of his ambition, that must be done which would utterly crush his fondest hopes.

We may not say of a certainty in what precise manner JEPHTHAH's vow was fulfilled. His daughter was allowed to go away for two menths among the mountains, and bewail her virginity; and from this fact some reason that, instead of being literally offered up as a burnt-offering, she was merely doomed to a life of celibacy. But even this was considered a sad fate indeed among Israelitish women, for they all held to the hope of being, by mother-hood, placed in the line of the Messiah which was to come. And it was especially sad for JEPHTHAH, as it would give the rulership into other lineage upon his death, which occurred six years thereafter.

The lesson of this Old Testament narrative is a vital one to-day. We see JEPHTHAHS everywhere about us, sacrificing all that which is dearest and best for ambition's sake. To accomplish one fond desire they make vows as foolish and reckless as was JEPHTHAH's vow of old, and that bring as sad and fearful results in the end. The very law of human life at present seems in a lamentable sense the law of sacrifice. It is the giving up of the sweetest and tenderest affections for something which profiteth not at all. It is the ignoring of those most purifying influences and aspirations, for the unsatisfying peace of an outward success. Over all merely worldly victories some shadow of JEPHTHAH's vow and sacrifice should rest, to teach what such victories, gotten at such a cost, really mean. They are the bitterest of Dead Sea apples, and have proved so to more JEPHTHAHS than we can number.

OUR Sabbath Evening is not alone a season of quiet, restful reflectiveness, but a season of sacred song. In the gathering twilight one softly intones, ''Sweet hour of prayer, sweet hour of prayer,'' and we all take up the tender words, and they tremble into a chorus, and so we sing ourselves into prayerfulness and pray on in melody with bowed hearts. ''JESUS, lover of my soul,'' another voice begins, later on, and every word of that dear hymn touches us to a deeper penitential love, and a sweeter trust in that Refuge for all our kind.

Mayhap there is silence for a little, when the final cadence has died away, and we sit musing upon the goodness of GOD in giving us songs so satisfying. Then, presently,—out of yonder corner where the home-mother sits—rise the strains of ''Rock of Ages, Cleft for Me,'' and musing swells into gladness in TOPLADY's fine old hymn. After the hymn is over, and while we still sit here in the twilight, we think of this man whose hymn we have sung, and fancy it would be pleasant to die as he died.

In the pleasant county of Devon, England, and in one of its sequestered passes, with a few cottages sprinkled over it, mused and sang AUGUSTUS TOPLADY. When a lad of sixteen, and on a visit to Ireland, he strolled into

a barn, where an illiterate layman was preaching recon-
ciliation to God through the death of His Son. The
homely sermon took effect, and from that moment the
gospel wielded all the powers of his brilliant and active
mind. Toplady became learned, but it was not so much
his learning that blessed us all, as his hymns.

During his last illness he seemed to lie in the very
vestibule of glory. To a friends inquiry he answered,
with sparkling eye, "Oh, my dear sir, I can not tell the
comforts I feel in my soul—they are past expression.
The consolations of God are so abundant that they leave
me nothing to pray for. My prayers are all converted
into praise. I enjoy a heaven already in my soul."
And within an hour of dying he called his friends, and
asked if they could give him up ; and when they said
they could, tears of joy ran down his cheeks as he added,
"Oh, what a blessing that you are made willing to give
me over into the hands of my dear Redeemer, and part
with me ; for no mortal can live after the glories which
God has manifested to my soul !" And thus he passed
away.

I SHALL BE SATISFIED.

I NEVER here may know content,
   Or feel a full, a perfect bliss ;
May never climb the long ascent
   And find the joy that here I miss ;
But somewhere, in the years to be,
   Beyond the portals opening wide
Across the lowly vale, for me,
   At length I shall be satisfied !

Be satisfied ! O, faith so sweet
   That helps me onward day by day !
That guides my weak and blinded feet
   Along the upward tending way !
It is the star that bright and clear
   Shines downward thro' my clouded night,
That has a tender, holy cheer
   Within its steady burning light.

Be satisfied ! Fly quickly, years,
   And bring that day of days the best,
When all the sickening doubts and fears
   Shall vanish from my anxious breast !
And waiting moments, whisper low.
   As far away these days recede,
Of purer pleasures I shall know,—
   Supplies that fill my every need.

Have patience, O my throbbing heart !
   The moments will not slowly creep ;

And life is only here a part
  Of one long, fitful, troubled sleep.
I shall awake sometime, Ah, yes !
  This slumber shall be put aside,
And in my Lord's fair comeliness
  I shall be fully satisfied !

PENALTIES FOR SIN.

THE law of compensation is just, and it is wide-reaching.   There is nothing born out of naught ; there is no
good or ill but has its recompense.   Patience hath its
reward   sooner   or   later ;   continuance   in   well-doing
finally works out an abundance of joy ; and persistence
in wickedness wins, sooner or later, the penalties which
it woos.

In so far as men accept grievous woes as penalties for
their transgressions, rather than as dark and incomprehensible afflictions, will they be profited and made better
thereby.   Losses and crosses, and trials and tribulations
are common to each of us, and they are not purposeless.
They are so common, indeed, that we forget what their
purpose may be, and are content only to weep over them.
We call them "dispensations of Providence," but with so
vague an idea of what a dispensation really is that the
term signifies nothing, and our recognition of it implies
simply that trust which receives because it cannot reject.

Dispensations of Providence are God's distributions of justice to men; and as justice abides ever in the law of compensation, each dispensation unto us is but our just due. The laborer is worthy of his hire; if he doeth evil his wages will be of evil. It is but natural, perhaps, that when some dearly-prized treasure is taken away from us, we should murmur in sore bitterness of spirit, and cry out against the great Dispenser. It is but natural, because we are human, and love for our kind is the deepest instinct of our humanity. But when we get a little way removed from our sorrow,—when it has become a thing of yesterday, as thank God sorrows will!—we shall see how the crushing of our love was altogether right, and how fully, by pride, or worldliness, or neglect of duty, or indifference to divine callings, we had earned what we have received.

We *shall* see this? Not certainly, but we ought to. We shall, if through saving grace our Christianity is not a name, but a breathing vitality,—if by the logic of love, spiritual and refining, and tending heavenward, we come to recognize Divine conclusions as altogether wise and righteous. And if we do not,—if for the treasure lost, and the hope unattained, and the joy taken from us, we continue to lament bitterly,—if, instead of a prayer, our soul sends up daily a plaint, and says to its God "Thou art unjust, and deal in vengeance rather than justice,"— then this our new and oft repeated sin will, of a certainty, bring its reward; either here, or in the long hereafter, we shall pay the penalty.

" So He bringeth them at last into their desired haven."

These were the words of the preacher's text one week ago to-night. RUTH says them over now, with a kind of gladness in her voice—dear, good, matronly RUTH, who does weary sometimes, as we all do, of the work done and to be done.

"I was disappointed with that sermon," she remarks. "I hoped it would be restful to us all : but it made so much of the struggle and storm of life, and so little of the calm and peace at the last. I would rather think of the peace."

"But we must think of the way to that, dear heart?"

" ' So *He bringeth* them ' is all the thought we need," she makes reply. "I care not what the way may be, with my hand in His ; I am surely safe, whatever storms may arise, with Him as pilot. I will not doubt that we shall reach the haven in His own good time."

"And you know what your ' desired haven ' is to be?"

"No, I do not," and she grows more thoughtful of countenance. "I am willing to trust that also, to Him. I am just a poor ignorant mariner, sailing an unknown sea for a port I never saw. I hail no vessel outward bound. None who sail thither ever come back. And yet I am certain it is a lovely country, because my GOD dwells there !"

"But God dwells also here on the earth?"

"Yes; and earth is lovely, when we see Him. The trouble is we only catch glimpses of Him, here; there, we shall behold Him ever face to face!"

She stops talking, and out of the silence, presently, some one sings:

> Face to face! O living Lord!
> This the sweetest, best reward
> Thro' the future aye shall be—
> Face to face, to gaze on Thee!

> Face to face! my longing eyes
> Wait the wondrous, glad surprise.
> Here the visions fade or tire,
> Grant me there, my one desire!

> Weak and tempted, faltering, faint,
> Hush my murmuring and complaint;
> Look in mercy here on me,
> That I there may look on Thee!

It is not enough that man be saved from final death, in the future. He needs salvation from himself in the present,—salvation from all those belittling influences within which may not send him to perdition at the last, but which cramp his Christianity, and dwarf his usefulness, and eat out all his manly nobleness.

AGAIN the twilight tender breathes
  Along the hillside slopes,
And earth in dreamy vestment wreathes
  Her promises and hopes ;
But through the gathering eventide
  A sweet voice sings to me—
"Let Faith through all the night abide,
  And wait the good to be.
There comes a day with dawn sublime :
The present is earth's twilight time !"

The song sinks deep my heart within ;
  I catch its inner thought ;
And all the years of darkest sin
  Are with new meaning fraught.
I see them as a misty haze,
  In which we blindly go,
With only stars above the maze
  We journey to and fro ;
And glad I sing—" A dawn sublime
At last will crown earth's twilight time !"

O doubt that broodeth over all !
  O wearing unbelief !
O woes that on the peoples fall !
  O universal grief !
Ye reign awhile, but not for long ;
  Our freedom comes at last,
And hearts will shout a victor's song
  O'er dangers haply passed.
Your night will wane ; a dawn sublime
Awaits beyond earth's twilight time !

THAT was a very touching little recital which one lady made in the prayer-meeting, a few evenings since. They had been talking of prayer—its efficacy and power.

"My father is a man of seventy," the lady said. "All his life he has been skeptical about religious things. He has been strictly moral, but yet more or less a skeptic. The other day I received a letter from him, saying he had changed his views of the Bible, and trusted he was now a follower of CHRIST. It was his mother's prayers, he declared, that brought him at the very last to GOD. They had always haunted him. He could never get quite free from their influence. And yet his mother died when he was only ten years old."

There is a sort of everlastingness about prayer—about prayers. Many a petition goes a lifetime unanswered, which finds its answer at the very close. The prayers of a mother live on in the life of a child. He may go far into sin, but he never can get wholly away from memory and the past. If in childhood he heard his mother plead with CHRIST for her loved one's soul, he will always feel his soul is worth caring for.

Ah, mothers! let your children hear you pray! If there be burdens to carry, and they press and weary you, and you faint utterly, do not forget to pray, even then.

You may tire of prayers never answered; you may grow impatient with GOD because of long delay; but think of this man of three score and ten, brought into CHRIST's love, after sixty intervening years, by the power of a mother's prayers. In GOD's good time all answers come.

THE UNDERLYING HOPE.

OTHER people than Christians have hopes,—hopes that are sweet and tender, and fondly cherished. This is not a hopeless world. There is some great good to come, for us all. There is a universal blessing somewhere in store : let us believe it and be glad.

But the tenderest and sweetest hopes, outside the one Great Hope of the Christian, are fleeting. How they come and go—sweet in their coming, sad in their going. How they fade into dreams, and are only remembered with a sigh. How they lead us up to some great height of happiness, and then drop us into the depths.

Only in the underlying Hope is there steadfastness. It never deceives. It never fails. They who build upon it have a firm foundation. It is broad as the needs of the broadest life ; it is deep as the eternities. It includes love undying, repose that no untoward influences can disturb, expectations that will by-and-by be fully met. It means so much more than we can understand : so much more than now, with our limited capacities, we can enjoy!

Blessed, indeeed, are they who have this Hope.   In their night seasons they shall see light.   In their sorrows there shall be cheer.   When the night comes down on those without this Hope, how dark it is!   And the nights come, to all.   It is day with us now, mayhap, but as surely as the day shines, the shadows will lengthen. We can not always be at the noontime.   Do we love?— the ones we love will die.   Do we possess?—our possessions will slip from our grasp.   Do we aspire?—we shall faint and fall, and the fever of aspiration will burn out, leaving us weak and helpless as a sick child.

Yes, the night seasons must come.   They are among the inevitables.   But they cannot absolutely darken the life of those who build upon the Underlying Hope. Ever since that sorrowful evening when CHRIST suffered in Gethsemane, for all who believe on Him there have been stars in the night, and a glad glimmer as of the dawn.   Do Christians ever give up in despair?   Then it is simply because they shut out the light, and close their eyes to its comfort.   There is for them no need to be groping in the dark.   All the cheer of all the ages is theirs to enjoy if they will.   The Hope that upheld a PAUL, and strengthened a STEPHEN, and sweetened the nature of a ST. JOHN, is ours now as it was theirs then,

FEED MY LAMBS.

" Lovest thou me?" He asked, of old,
   Who loved all men with a love divine.
Over and over the love was told,
   And over and over He named a sign.
" Feed my lambs, " was the one command ;—
   This of love was the sign and test;
For through the work of a willing hand
   Will throb the warmth of a loving breast.

" Feed my lambs!"   There were lambs unfed,
   Though then the flock it was young and small ;
And though to but one the words were said,
   They were meant for us, they were meant for all.
And now far over the pastures wide
   His sheep are scattered—the weak and strong—
And some have never a shepherd guide,
   Are weak and worn, and the way is long.

" Lovest thou me?" He asks to-day,
   Of many who walk unheeding by :
" Yea, Lord, Thou knowest it," still we say :
   " Then feed my lambs !" is His warning cry.
And still they faint in the noontide's heat,
   Still amid hunger and thirst they go,—
Shepherd of Love, in Thy care complete,
   Lead them to fields that no hunger know !

CHRISTIAN PATIENCE.

"IT is hard to wait!"

RUTH has been reading again the little poem we read a few evenings since, entitled "The Service of Waiting."

"I want to see results. I want to know my life means something to GOD, by seeing He uses it. I am willing to do, but what has GOD for me?"

There are many who feel as RUTH feels. The natural longing of us all is for results. The common cry of the Soul is, "What has GOD for me?"

Because we are all possessed of the belief that we are to do and accomplish visible things. We all like to think there is before us some work ordained of GOD, which, with GOD's help, we are to perform. Very few look upon a life without results upon the world as worth living.

And we mistake, often, in waiting for what will never come. Having fixed our mind on some definite thing, come certain line of doing, we come to think GOD means no work for us because He does not provide as we expect. We ask the question, "What has GOD for us?" with a complaint. What we most desire has not come up for careful effort and accomplishment; we are disappointed and would find fault.

But we must be patient. We must exercise genuine Christian patience. Well, how does Christian patience differ from patience in general ? First of all, in having a hope in it—the Great Hope, that is to gladden the world. Having a hope, it is not a patience of philosophy, of willing to endure, of hardened stoicism. It is a patience of trust. Faith lights it up continually.

Superadded to this, it is a patience of searching. The heart in close sympathy with CHRIST will wait patiently for the GOD-appointed work, but it will not wait idly, complainingly, and say "GOD brings naught for my doing." It will search every day, to see if perchance, in some unlooked-for manner, the mission has not come unannounced, unsuspected. It will refuse no offered opportunity. It will accept, in all earnestness, the proffered service, and serve as patiently as it had waited.

O Lord, is heart of mine like this ?—
In careful search lest it should miss
The labor Thou wouldst ask of me ?
Or do I wait and long to see
Some special work before me set,
And fold my hands while I forget
That in this waiting of to-day,
And in this that I call delay,
The Master's voice is sounding near,
" Why idly are ye standing here ?"

"SAUL s agony should not be waited for nor desired, if GOD gives one LYDIA's open heart."

Thus said the preacher this morning, speaking of the manner of conversion, and in the saying he touched very wisely a point which has troubled many souls.

The being born again seems so hard a thing. But why? Because we make it so. We magnify its difficulties. We see more to get over than really exists. We hold change of heart to be a most marvelous transition, when in fact it is very simple—surprisingly simple, sometimes.

There are few cases like that of SAUL. Few indeed are there who from midnight gloom, impending days together, emerge into supreme splendor of light. It is seldom that GOD meets a man so suddenly on the way as He met SAUL; and none should expect to realize SAUL's remarkable experience in their own history.

LYDIA furnishes an excellent example for all such as await some profound, agonizing conviction. She waited for nothing ; she simply believed, with her whole heart, nd this heart-felt belief was the being born again. The new birth is a change, certainly; but it is a change from unbelief and doubt to perfect trust and faith. There can be no change without faith. The man's withered arm was not restored until it was stretched forth. A belief that CHRIST can heal the soul, alone makes the healing possible. And when we have this belief it is idle, unwise, to wait long and anxiously for some harrowing sense of pain and sin. A degree of self-smiting there must be, but the degree differs in intensity in different cases.

So the preacher did well to mention SAUL and LYDIA to us in the same breath—to show us how widely separated in character conversions may be, and yet be each acceptable in the Divine sight.

SELLING OUR BIRTHRIGHTS.

THERE are many ESAUS. Of the multitudes of men who go up and down among us, how many are there who have not sold their birthrights?

Notwithstanding the fall, there is a birthright for every one. Manhood is the noblest heritage which can accrue to being. Purity, honor and truth were not all upyielded when the first man sinned. In these each man has still a share. Of these, alas! thousands are daily selling their portion for a mess of pottage!

ESAU and JACOB of old were types of two great classes that were to exist long after,—the one weak, lustful and foolish; the other sharp far-sighted, grasping. And so long as ESAUS remain, there will be JACOBS to profit by their weakness, their improvident. So long as one man stands ready to make over all that is best and truest in his life and character, his fellow will be at hand eager to receive the trust and to use it to his own selfish advancement.

But are we all sufficiently generous to give up self utterly for the sake of others? Is our generosity wise? Just such spiritual loss as was ESAU's may not be ours, in selling our birthrights, for there is no Messiah to come in our genealogical line; but there is an awful loss, nevertheless. And what is the gain? Your mess of pottage may be for the moment very tempting; does its flavor last? Partaking of it, do you see your birthright pass into the hands of another and feel satisfied?

Oh, these messes of pottage! They are of Satan's own mixing. They stand ready everywhere. What are they? We cannot tell. Some delightful dalliance may make up one; some lustful indulgence may savor forth in another; some unholy amusement, some selfish propensity, some secret sin, some open-transgression, some destroying desire, may comprise another. But at their best they are only pottage, and miserable compensation for that which they purchase. Is it not a little strange that men ordinarily keen at a bargain make such a losing thing of it in selling themselves?

THE SONG OF MIRIAM.

OF all that singers e'er have sung
　　Since singing first began,
No strains have gladder, clearer rung
From human heart, from human tongue,
　　Than where the Red Sea ran —

Where horse and rider fierce and wild
　　By God were overthrown :
Where He upon His children smiled,
And swift their foes to wreck beguiled
　　By waves His breath had blown.

" For He hath triumphed gloriously !"
　　And " Sing ye to the Lord ! "
The singer chanted by the sea :
And glad as anthem of the free
　　Rang out her clear accord.

Dear singer of the ancient time !—
　　Her timbrel echoes still
Adown the ages.　Sweet, sublime,
Above the din of doubt and crime,
　　We catch its hopeful thrill.

Within our Edom weary years
　　We wander sore beset ;
The host of Egypt oft appears ;
We yield at last to fate and fears,
　　To grieving and regret.

But waiting there in doubt and dread,
   Our own Red Sea beside,
Some ray of silver sunlight, shed
From God's clear sky, shines on our head,
   And gloom is glorified !

And listning then we hear the song
   They sang that time of old,
When God was faithful, swift and strong
To help the Right, to crush the Wrong ,
   And faith finds deeper hold.

For God is God to-day, as then .
   He minds His Israel :
Above all battlings fierce of men
He waits in patient power, as when
   The host Egyptian fell.

Dear singer of that distant day !—
   Her Edom had its springs
Of bitter waters by the way :
And we by Marah's side may stay
   Oft in our wanderings ;

But though the way be long and sore,
   This side the Promised Land,
Some song of cheer forevermore
May thrill us, that we sang before
   We came to desert sand.

Some yesterday of song we knew,—
   Some hour of joy and praise
After a Red Sea's journey through
To peace ; and God to-day is true,
   However dark the ways :

And just beyond the wilderness
    Our Land of Promise lies ;
Its plenty we shall soon possess ;
Its beauty shall our morrow bless
    With comforting surprise !

THE MASTER TRUTH.

TRUTH has been master since the Master's first preaching of it. It will be master in all time to come. It can not be crushed. The defection of followers and supporters can not dangerously weaken it. It is upheld by living divine grace.

What does it matter, then, if some one fall whom the world has looked up to as eminently a disciple of Truth? Falls are common. Men are but human, and the greatest may be most human. The greatest may sink into ways of sin and shame. But if one or a thousand great upholders of CHRIST's Gospel lapse from the true path, shall we be foolish enough to think that Gospel suffers irreparable harm?

When this dear religion of ours had few supporters, it stood up under defection and betrayal greater than can possibly befall it now. There was JUDAS—one of the favored Twelve. A cruel blow was his ; and yet the new faith survived. There was PETER—he was tempted and he fell ; and yet the new faith lived on, and grew marvelously in the hearts of men.

A man may have much of the grace of GOD in his heart, and for all this he may yield to sudden tempting. A man may profess love for CHRIST, and kiss him to betrayal. Is he the annihilator of our faith? Far from it. He falls; but honest men everywhere will simply pity his weakness or scorn his falsity. They will not say that CHRIST is a myth, or His Gospel a fiction. And if they were to say it, what then? Fools have said the same these hundreds of years, and men have fallen from purity time and again, and yet CHRIST is not a myth, and His Gospel is not a fiction, and people go on believing.

It is sad—very sad—to see any one betray his faith. The influence of such betrayal may be wide-reaching, and the injury done may be great. But to say that betrayal is terribly disastrous, is idle talk. There can never be a worse, a more awful betrayal than that of JUDAS; and doubtless the weak and troubled disciples thought it disaster dire. Instead, it held the world's hope. It wrought out the best that life can know. It was a never-ending blessing just begun.

'Shall we then excuse betrayal and palliate a fall, because irretrievable ruin does not come of it? By no means. To fall is to sin; to betray is criminal. Truth is sinned against in either case. JUDAS betrays himself when he betrays and turns against his CHRIST. He must pay the penalty. If only himself be hurt, even, there is no excuse, since no man may excusably sin against himself. And always the sin reaches past the sinner, past the second party sinned against, and harms community. That it is not a fatal harm, matters not, though it is the

one comforting thing Christians should remember ever—
that no man's weakness mortally weakens the church of
CHRIST. Such has never been the case ; such never can
be the case. The church of CHRIST is not founded upon
man ; does not depend upon man for its continuance,
and can not be overthrown by man.

CHRIST'S COMPASSION.

PERHAPS there is no more really comforting thought,
in relation to CHRIST's compassionate love, than that it
was discriminative. "CHRIST loved men in the mass,"
said the preacher this morning; "but He also loved
men as individuals."

We have numerous illustrations of this discriminating
regard. Among them all, none is so sweetly tender as
that of the widow of Nain. CHRIST was upon the highway, accompanied by many followers. He met another
company, and their errand was evident. They were going to a burial. It was not an unusual thing to meet
such a sad procession.

Yet to our SAVIOUR it was an unusual case, common
as it might seem to all about Him. Here was a woman
following a loved one to the grave ; and this was sad indeed, and in a general way was sufficient to call forth
sympathy. Bnt it was worse than this. "She was a

widow." She had followed a bier, before. She had wept for her companion; now, alas! she must weep for her sole support—her only son! and this was saddest of all.

It was, indeed, a case where discriminating comfort would not fail of expression and endeavor. The great heart of JESUS went out in tender compassion. His Divine power found manifestation in the command "Arise!" And the sorrowing mother found a Friend where least she expected one, a Helper when to human ken help was no longer possible. What a joy was hers! How she must have gone back rejoicing, who had come from her home in tears!

It is ever with the needy, whose faith is strong, as it was with the widow of Nain. CHRIST will not fail in His discriminative compassion. On the highway of life He meets men and women now, as He met them ages ago, and knows their peculiar want. We like to believe that when blind BARTIMEUS called out to Him from the roadside, "Thou son of David, have mercy on me!" our SAVIOUR knew him for the sightless man he was, and not simply as one of the common mass, voicing a common need. To the blind of to-day His ear is open still, and He will not fail to hear. Hearing He will not fail to bless, and blessing, the needy shall go forth rejoicing, who now weep on the way.

IT is an evening for tears. One year ago to-night—or was it two, or three, or five?—you wept over a dear face waxing cold, and dropped a hand out of yours from which love's answering pressure had fled. How well you remember it! Will you ever forget? Would you ever, if you could? Would you even now put from you these memories so sadly sweet, that bring dimness to your eyes and fresh sorrow to your heart?

You thought the first pang of separation hard ; you feel scarcely different after all these months or years of loneliness. And yet you have now none of those bitter, fault-finding feelings against GOD which took possession of you at the beginning. You have come to realize somewhat of GOD's kindliness even through His afflicting—somewhat of His great overbrooding love and wide-reaching sympathy.

In the first overwhelming of your grief you thought hard things of your CREATOR, hard things of your SAVIOUR. You said in your heart—"He is but an indifferent SAVIOUR who does not save me from this depth of woe." You know now how much you wronged CHRIST. Indifferent? You could hardly say that of Him again, though you stood by another open grave. Indifferent? You read one little verse in your Bible, as you have read it many times of late, and you acknowledge how very human our SAVIOUR was—how His heart went out in a common sorrow with those who were sorrowful.

"JESUS wept."

Thank GOD that there is such a verse in the Book of books! If CHRIST had been divine alone, we might never have had it. But those two words tell the whole story of His humanity. Because weeping is such a common lot, it was necessary, so it seems, that CHRIST should weep also. If not necessary, it was fitting. And the fact that our SAVIOUR wept with those who wept, brings Him nearer to us all evermore. No proof is needed to establish CHRIST's divinity, even though men have thought it their duty to write books full of argument; there might have been call for proof to substantiate His humanity, without this fact.

So you accept the story so briefly told, as it is accepted by many another, and your sorrow is not so sharp a thing as once you held it. Because JESUS wept, weeping is somehow sanctified. Grief is not so crushing since you know that He felt it, even in the very phase so familiar to you. And through your tears you are thankful for a tearful SAVIOUR, and you feel that GOD who gave such an one must be, and indeed is, very good, though He smite you.

THE FATHER'S VOICE.

O STUBBORN heart of mine, be still !
   God speaks to you, to day ;
In silence wait His holy will—
   In silence Him obey.

Your sore complaint forget awhile,
   Your longing and your pain ;
And in the sweetness of His smile
   A perfect peace obtain.

So near to Him, O heart of mine !
   That we His voice can hear :
Our being is a thing divine,
   With love its heavenly cheer.

For love is in His every tone,
   And in His presence shines ;
He speaks in love, and love alone
   His every act inclines.

Then listen to His loving call,
   O heart of mine, I pray !
Let doubt that broodeth over all
   By Him be chased away!

Let Faith a cherished guest abide,
   Where unbelief has dwelt,
And patience tarry by her side,
   And Love all discord melt.

And so as pass the waning days,
    At length, O heart of mine !
Your song shall be a psalm of praise,
    Where song is all divine !

AN APPROPRIATING FAITH.

"IT was a good sermon from a good text," says RUTH
to-night, referring to the morning's discourse. " ' The
LORD is my shepherd, I shall not want.' I was glad when
the preacher chose such words as these, for a hope and a
comfort. I was gladder yet, even, when he showed how
DAVID's was only like what every follower should feel
now—an appropriating faith. The LORD was more than
a shepherd to Israel's king—*his* shepherd; He is more
than a shepherd to you and to me—even *our* shepherd.
And because He is ours, in this sense of personal appro-
priation, we shall not want."

RUTH's face is not visible, in the twilight, but we fancy
gladness glows upon it, and we know that her voice
tiembles with a thrill of joy.

Ah, yes ! The faith of the Psalmist should typify our
faith to-day. It was as sweetly personal as if DAVID knew
he and GOD made up the world. The same individual
trust and acceptaticn should dwell in us. Why not?
Has the LORD changed in all these years ? No ; He is
the Everlasting. Have our relations to Him altered? No;

we are His people to the end of time,—His people, and the sheep of His pasture. As He led those of old, so likewise shall He lead us. The still waters, the pastures green—lo! these are unchanging as the Eternal Father, and to them we shall as surely come as came the weary ones who knew them at last henceforth and forevermore.

And it was a rare assurance that grew out of DAVID's appropriating faith—"I shall not want." Here was no shadow of doubt, no thought of questioning, nothing but a strong, sweet certainty, to rest upon and be upheld by. The same certainty may be appropriated·and enjoyed by us. Why not? Since GOD is *our* GOD—since a risen SAVIOUR rose for *us*, as well as for the great world at large—since we are individually responsible for taking hold or letting go of a faith that binds us to an individual LORD—so should we realize that all the fruits of a personal faith are ours as truly as though none other ever shared them, as though in GOD's clear vision no other mortal stood.

There is a blind, helpless faith, that believes without tasting, or testing, or knowing,—a vague trust in abstract truths, and a weak recognition of comprehensive Omniscience without any positive comprehension at all. It confesses GOD as the Supreme Ruler, but knows nothing of Him as the Shepherd who knows His sheep. It prays to GOD as a wise and beneficent CREATOR, but never tenderly supplicates Him as the one FATHER and FRIEND who sees every heart, appreciates every want, is lovingly mindful of each individual need. DAVID's was a faith wiser and more helpful. If our faith be truly wise, and of the best type, we shall appropriate and know GOD as none other exactly can, and He shall be to us, in some subtle sense, what He is to no other trusting soul.

IMPETUOUS CHRISTIANITY.

PETER was the impetuous apostle. We all know how his impetuosity cropped out, at times,—how he was most ready to declare love for his Master, then the first to deny Him. It was an inherent fault in his nature. He flared up at a spark. As susceptible to sleep on that memorable night of the Agony as his fellow disciples, he was prompt enough on the succeeding morning to cut off the ear of one of the band whom JUDAS led to the betrayal. His acts were as impetuous as his faith, and this came near to causing his death on an occasion familiar to all.

And PETER the impetuous was the type of a large class of Christians to come after him. Faith, belief, devotion, action, were with him a matter of impulse ; and they are so still with very many. Perhaps the proportion of impulsive faith, belief, devotion and service is as great to-day among CHRIST's followers as it was in the day of His ministry. Warmed by an atmosphere of loving nearness to GOD, thrilled by the prayers of faithful ones, many are eager to declare their fervent affection,—to asseverate stoutly that a denial of their LORD is impossible. But out amid the scorners, where CHRIST is jeered at and mocked, where to cling to Him may be to suffer contempt and ill-treatment, the impulse of denial is as ready as any other, and the denial is most emphatic.

Impulsive service is a poor service, at best. Its good effects are neutralized by the cold seasons intervening, when all devotion is forgotten, all faith apparently dead. But is impulsive service rare? Is it not part of almost every Christian life?—the bane of every Christian church? We draw the picture strong, possibly; but it does seem to us that Christian endeavor is largely characterized by impulse. We do much for a little time, when strongly moved, then relapse into inertia and discontent, if not utter carelessness. Our charity flows out to bless the needy only when melted to a white heat by external fires. Giving is not a matter of principle, but of impulse; doing springs not from an underlying purpose to serve GOD and our fellows, but is the result of outside influences, bearing so powerfully upon us for the time being that we cannot resist.

All good impulses should be cherished,—all will concede that. But life should not be all impulse,—nervous and uncertain. And our following after CHRIST should not be like unto PETER's, "afar off."

7

UNREST.

O GOD of peace ! soothe me to inner calm !
　　This wearying unrest
　　So racks and wounds my breast
I long for Thine own sweet anointing balm !

To feel Thy fingers touching all my care
　　To tenderness of peace,
　　Would make my longings cease :
O Father ! bend Thine ear and hear my prayer !

I hold so much of every earthly bliss
　　I should not e'er complain ;
　　And yet I pine in pain
For some dear blessing that I want, and miss.

I can not name it, Lord ; I do not know
　　If it should come to me
　　That I could clearly see
It was the blessing I had prayed for so.

So blind am I ; so vaguely and so dim
　　Is my desire defined
　　As yet within my mind ;
And yet I fancy it is known to Him !

Then fill, O Lord ! my emptiness of heart ;
　　My weary longings still
　　With Thine own holy will,
And grant that peace which shall no more depart !

COURTING SIN.

WE cannot avoid being tempted. In some form or other the spirit of evil comes to us every hour of our lives, with his magnificent promises. If we listen to them, half smilingly, are we not really courting sin? To go voluntarily to baleful influences, and put ourselves in their power, is little worse than to give ourselves over to those influences, without effort to the contrary, when they come to us. There is no excuse for half the defeats we meet with while endeavoring to walk uprightly. We surrender to temptation with never an arm upraised in defense. With not even a whispered "Get thee behind me, Satan," do we meet the tempter. And yet we bemoan our sinfulness; we make weak resolves to stand up more manfully in the future. All this is well. Repentance is very essential. But unless we cease tacitly courting sin by receiving it kindly when it visits us, of what avail are all our bemoanings, our tears, and our resolutions? Our visitors measure their stay by the character of their reception, and sin is no less sharp-sighted than they.

Then it is wiser to put sin behind us, always, rather than let it stand before us as an equal. The language our SAVIOUR used, when tempted, has a deeper significance than we are wont to give it. He said "Get thee *behind* me." And why *behind* ? Was it not to be wholly out of sight? Sin is hardly ever without a glamour over it, concealing its deformity, oftentimes rendering it absolutely beautiful. Satan may have a cloven foot, and the *et ceteras* commonly credited to him, but he is frequently exceeding fair to look upon. And the heart receives its impressions too often through the eyes. On that account it is dangerous, in the extreme, long to look evil in the face. Unless we voluntarily bid it get behind us, away from our seeing, it may become as an angel of light, blinding our vision completely.

And alas! how often our thought plays truant, and goes off kite-flying, like the veriest idler, in beautiful fields where all beauty hides a secret sting ! Into those lovely reaches we follow, no longer waiting for sin to come to us that we may be won, but going out after it, though we scarcely realize this, and wooing it in its own chosen haunts. And we go, and go again, until the way becomes worn and familiar, and the beauties throw off their outward seeming and pierce us with their sharp, biting realities. Then, wounded and sick at heart, we feel that it is not enough to pray " Lead us not into temptation," but that we must continually and in all earnestness declare " Get thee *behind* me, Satan ! "

"AND THEN?"

WE remember reading, years ago, of a man who was so sparing of his words that he seldom uttered more than two consecutively, and consequently was known as "Two Words." Favorites of his, and most often made use of, were these, short and questioning,—"*And then?*"

Every man, woman and child utters them frequently,— they are indeed the text of many a hope, many a promise, many a prayer. Childhood will grow out of its childishness, *and then*—all the joys and successes of manhood will gladden it. Youth will step out from its youthful annoyances, *and then*—will come only halcyon days, full of sunlight and song, and glad fulfillments. Manhood will brush away the clouds that envelop it, *and then*—the long awaited rewards will surely be realized in maturer years. Manhood's prime may wear itself out in noble endeavors, but Old Age will reap the fruits, *and then*— content will render the hours peacefully sweet. Old Age will be ended by-and-by, *and then*—

And then—what?

It is not enough that we dream over the two words,— that we use them as pleasant agencies to conjure up brightness for the future. To paint beautiful pictures of the "Good time coming" is well, because none have a right to shut the sunlight out of their lives, and the sunlight streams in ever through the open door of To-mor-row ; but to shut our eyes to our possible destiny,—to look resolutely away from a destiny that must be inevit-ably ours,—that is not well.   It is the height of folly, or else the climax of cowardice.

Thousands are dancing through life thinking lightly of the morrow, with *"And then"* upon their lips, but never repeating it in its deep and solemn suggestiveness.   Poor fools, that make a minuet of the week, and glide down it careless and unconcerned, for them, as for all others, there will come a Saturday night with its silent hush, and the sun will go down, and the stars will come out, and the soul will remember itself—*and then*—

As we have each our by-and-bys, that we fill with those things we love best, so is there for all one great common By-and-By, and it is surer than those little ones we think most of.   Who says "by-and-by" with a thought of all its meaning?   We hang upon being as by a thread, and yet we plan with an "I *will*," as though the future were ours to do with as we please.   And some day we shall see our mistake.   Some day we shall say "I will," and our wills shall be as mere breaths ; and it shall be then, O Father, "as *Thou* wilt ;" and we shall close our eyes to all around us and go out somewhere by a way we know not—*and then ?*

"COME UNTO ME!"

"COME unto me!" I stand far off and lonely,
    And hear the words so sweet.
Dear Saviour! but to meet Thy greeting only
      Grant me swift feet!

"Come unto me!" The air is full of voices
    That call me loudly hence.   .
Help me to feel that most Thy call rejoices
      With recompense.

I see before me, onward ever luring,
    The prizes rich and rare ;
But each shall fade. Thine only is enduring,
      Beyond compare.

Thine only. What Thou freely givest ever,
    The thing no man can earn ;
For which no pain, nor any long endeavor,
      Can make return.

Thine only—now ; but when I fly to meet Thee,
    In love, as Thou dost call,
Then as with tender, broken heart I greet Thee,
      My own, my all !

Thy Rest ! Dear Saviour, make me for it eager,
    And never satisfied
With all that I may win, so poor and meager,
      From Thy dear side !

As we sit in the twilight, a solemn silence falls upon us all.

"Be still, and know that I am God!" Ruth by-and-by quotes. And then she adds:

"Is silence just another name for submission, I wonder? Last evening Mrs. Bird came in, and we talked of her great loss. The dear boy she buried a year ago lives freshly yet, in her grief. She can not give him up. She will not believe that the Lord did well in taking him away. It grieved me to hear her talk, and I have been troubled about it all day."

"She is not an obedient scholar in the school of sorrow," one of us makes reply. "'Be still and *learn*,' might be said wisely to her. We hear many things in our moments of quiet, which miss us in the hours of our speech. We can not both speak and hear at once."

"True," answers Ruth, "but have you quite caught the meaning of those words I quoted? As I see it, we are not left to *learn* that God is God ; we are simply to be still and *know*. There is something fairly divine in the assumption which this command implies. In twilight times, or times of darkness coming over the soul, we may just keep silent and rest in a sure knowledge. In our submissive stillness we shall know what by no common process of accquirement could we learn. To be restful before God, as I take the thought into my heart, is absolutely to know Him.

"And the knowledge will never make us glad, I fear," she continues, "if we do not feel subdued to perfect peace. Nobody can find out God by searching, or by scientific investigation, or by noisy discussion. He is not revealed to men through visible demonstrations. It is only in soul-quiet that the soul, looking upward, grows wise. We have so much turmoil in life, and we spend so many days and years in perpetual unrest, no wonder we fail to know God as we ought. I prize the twilight hours more than once I did, for their quietude, and their holy intimacies. God does come near to quiet souls, I am certain. We can know Him if we will but be still, and let Him visit us in blessed recognition."

"You hold, then, by your personal relation to Him?"

"Why not? If I am to know Him, it must be a personal knowledge, made possible through a personal intimacy. For me to know God is to know Him for myself, and of myself, and not to become a mere partaker of another's knowledge. I may not profit by another's obedient silence, while my own soul cries out in doubting complaint. I could not teach Mrs. Bird of my happy knowledge, when she cherished the turmoil of her grief, and would not be still that she might know. Whoever believes may enjoy the blessed certainty of knowing, but before knowing, in the truest, sweetest sense, he must hush all his strivings of soul, quiet all his troubling fears, and come, so, before knowledge, into peace. And the best of it is that God will help him to do this, that so doing he *may* know!"

In the prayer meeting the other night we were considering the subject of Patience. And one brother remarked that we ought to be more patient with ourselves—that having done a wrong thing, and properly confessed to GOD and self that it was wrong, we should not continue to upbraid self, and be miserable. Then he cited the case of a little child, in illustration.

The little one had been guilty of some misdeed. She had asked her father's forgiveness, and it had been freely granted. Still she seemed a little ill at ease. "Have you told GOD how you feel about it?" her father asked. No, she had not, but she went away by herself, and pretty soon returned, satisfied, her countenance all aglow. "Is it all right now?" the parent inquired. "O, yes!" was her answer.

She had confessed the fault, and she *lost no time in beginning again.* She did not go about with a sober, dejected countenance, bewailing her sin, making her life miserable on account of it. Even so should we be patient with ourselves. We sin often. If, after the sin is confessed and repented of, we go around for hours or days together reproaching ourselves, encouraging impatience toward ourselves, we sin again. We should lose no time in reproaches, which ought to be spent in beginning a new course of life. It does not mend the wrong to put our souls in perpetual penance for it. Better that we atone for it by a speedy setting about the course of right. Better that we take up a vigorous line of good conduct, than that we sit down idly and sorrow over the unhappy slip.

There is a lesson here which many should heed. Healthful Christian life is not promoted by brooding over, and doing mental penance for, the sins of the past. Before us there is a work to be done. Let us do it. What though we failed once, or even many times? The failures do not excuse us from fresh attempting. The bitterest reproaches we can heap upon self will not expiate for faults or failures of the days gone by. Let us be good to ourselves, then, and having properly and freely repented of that which we can not recall, let the dead bury its dead. So shall we live happier lives. So shall we be better fitted for all that each day brings.

RELIGION is belief in GOD and His revelations; an acceptance of the Divine as ruling over the Human ; a faith in the spiritual as working in and through the material. And to be religious is to acknowledge GOD's power and man's weakness, human need and Divine helpfulness; and to confess, in heart and life, that the sin of the fall is only annulled in the expiation of the Cross.

THE TOUCH OF FAITH.

O LORD! Thou walkest in this earthly press,
    As once Thou dids't before ;
Thy presence hath the same sweet power to bless
    That it possessed of yore.
Then let me come anear, O Lord, I pray!
    Nor my one wish condemn ;
Let me, like her of old, approach to-day,
    And touch Thy garment's hem !

My deepest want Thy healing grace can meet,—
    O grant that grace to give !
My poor unfinished life Thou shalt complete
    If I but touch and live !
I faint amid the many striving sore ;
    I fear me lest I fall ;
O turn Thine ear, dear Saviour, I implore
    And hear my pleading call !

O touch of faith ! I feel its healing power !
    My weakness groweth strong !
I rise renewed in life, this favored hour ;
    I praise Him in my song !
Dear soul-sick ones, behind Him closely press !
    He gladly healeth them
Whose faith can see Him through all earthliness
    And touch His garment's hem !

PSALMS IN THE NIGHT.

THE singing hearts are ever a blessing unto themselves. A song is joy-giving. He who can sing sweetly in the undertone of his inner nature, carries a rare pleasure with him always. Hard things appear to him easy ; heavy burdens seem light ; sorrow knocks often, it may be, but often goes away, seldom enters.

And when it does enter—when the clouds come and the sunlight is hidden—when the soul walks down into the night and sees never a star ; what then? Ah! then thrice blest is the singing heart. If it can sing psalms at such a time, the stars *will* shine. Dawn will quicker come, the sunlight sooner re-appear.

Sweetest of all songs are the psalms in the night. DAVID sang with the most touching tenderness when in the gloom of deepest affliction. The heart may wail a *miserere* over its dead or its dying, but even that will be sadly sweet, and will have a hope in it. The saddest song is better than none, because it *is* a song.

Every song soothes and uplifts. It is just possible that a song is as good as a prayer. Indeed, a song of the pure kind recognized in Scripture, is akin to a petition, while it is also in the spirit of thanksgiving. The "sweet singer of Israel" wedded his sincerest prayers to melody, and wafted them upward on the night air from his throbbing heart.

Through God's grace we can all sing psalms in the night. Whatever brings the shadows, we need not be wholly surrounded by them. We can sing under the stars ; or, if they be hid, until they come out and smile down upon us, and cheer us to a gladder strain. There are dark nights for us all ; we are in them now, or have just found the dawn, or, perchance, are just entering the twilight. But there is a psalm for every over-creeping gloom ; and if the heart but take it up and chant it, the dreariness will surely vanish, and there will come in its stead hope and light and cheering warmth, and we shall grow glad again with the morning.

"NO NIGHT THERE."

O DREARINESS of earth ! O mocking pain !
    O day to darkness going !
    You hold but little in your empty showing ;
The end of all will be my greatest gain.
    There is within my limited foreknowing
For all your want and woe a kindly bane.

The ways of earth are dark ; the sunset lies,
    Unrobed of all its beauties,
    A shadow black and chill o'er all our duties,
And shutting out the smiling of the skies.
    Our better nature in the shadow mute is,
Or speaks but faintly through some quick surprise.

At intervals, perhaps, may clearly shine
    The stars, in friendly gleaming,
    As if to woo forgetfulness in dreaming,
And drown the earthly in the half divine ;
    Yet memory sleeps only in our seeming,
And consciousness breathes on, but makes no sign.

Our souls beneath the darkness sit alone
    In solitary places,
    And keenly scan the few by-passing faces,
In hope some newer light has outward shone ;
    But find thereof no sweetly cheering traces,
For yet is the all-perfect day unknown.

It waits somewhere beyond the evening hills,—
    That day without an ending.
    Pray God our steps are thither ever tending !
Its glory on our vision bursts and thrills,
    The rarest radiance through the darkness sending,
As dreams of dawn appear when fancy wills.

O endless day !   O triumph over night !
    O radiant glory rarest !
    Of earthly dreams thou art the best and fairest,
And I shall drink of thy supreme delight !
    I know that God for all my being carest ;
I know His sunshine yet shall bless my sight !

" No night there ! "   Shall I ever sadly miss
    The stars above me glowing ?
    What answer has my limited foreknowing ?
Some subtle prescience tells me only this :
    The stars within my crown, effulgence throwing,
Will satisfy me through an endless bliss !

Now, when the tendency of all things earthly is materialistic, it is perhaps not strange that there exists a desire to materialize spiritual things, and to make of Heaven only another earth, possessed of every circumstance known here except sin. But there is danger in this attempted materializing; and if such speculation be carried too far, results may prove sad indeed. However much we may want to know what lies beyond the grave, and just what that Heaven is like to which many of us hope sometime to go, curious queryings concerning it will avail us nothing. To human knowledge God has set a limit. "Thus far shalt thou go, and no farther," is the limitation; and the "thus far" is the grave. Through the green curtain of the sod we may not peer. Whatever awaits beyond that,—whatever of detail or surroundings, —we shall know only when the green curtain swings outward for us to enter.

And yet God has given us some beautiful foreshadowings of Heaven,—some outlines of the picture, to be filled in hereafter. They are sufficient for faith; they ought to answer all doubtful speculations of every kind. "For we know that when He shall appear we shall be like Him." It is possible to see in these words an existence quite different from that some recent writers presume the good will enjoy when they have put aside mortality. It is diffcult to believe Him as taking part in very material pleasures ; and if we are to be "like Him," we shall hardly cling to what we here count our chief joys. The peace and gladness of Heaven *may* spring from the using of earthly appliances, with our natures purified, and the using thereby rendered spiritual ; but we prefer to suppose that in the Better Land there will be found better agencies of happiness, and that, taking on immortality, we shall take on immortal surroundings.

"I shall be satisfied when I awake with Thy likeness." Here is the only picture of Heaven that is necessary to our trust while yet on earth. "I shall be *satisfied!*" This, with nothing added, would indeed be Heaven,— satisfaction. No more vague unrest ; no more anxious longings after something out of reach ; no more doubt, no more pain. The promise of a full and final content should be our sweet assurance through all strugglings,— all inclinations to doubt, or speculate upon, the life immortal. Let us not wonder whether the content will come through one means or another. It is enough that it *will* come ; and that in it and of it we shall find heavenly rest, and that joy which shall compensate for every earthly ill.

RUTH read the first chapter of Ecclesiastes aloud, this afternoon, and kept on until she read the whole book through. When she had finished the reading, one of us said—

"After all, SOLOMON was wrong. Life is *not* merely a vanity and a vexation of spirit. The wise man spoke unwisely. He had not given life a fair test."

Now, as the twilight deepens, we think over the Preacher's words, and say quietly to ourselves, Yes, SOLOMON was wrong. His sweeping declaration, "Vanity of Vanities, all is vanity," is not true. Life is more than a vanity.

And one of the reasons why we think SOLOMON was wrong, lies in the fact that a later Preacher taught so differently. There was born a babe, in Bethlehem of Judea—born not of the purple, but cradled in the manger, and brought up amid the disciplines of life. His youth was not passed in the enervating atmosphere of luxury. He knew what manly labor was. Doubtless he stood at the carpenter's bench at least a part of those thirty years before his preaching began.

And when at length he spoke to that narrow Judean world, and through that to the wide brotherhood of man, what a different ring had his words from those of the wise

man of old! "Blessed are the poor; blessed are they
that mourn ; blessed are the meek ; blessed are they that
do hunger and thirst;" blessed, blessed, blessed—in
what? In that which was only vanity? We can not believe it. Blessed in some life to come? That also, beyond question ; but before that, blessed here. The
present life is but a preparation for the life hereafter.
Think you the preparation would be all vanity, when the
ultimate end is to be so real it can never know ending?
"Man dies as the beast dieth," said the complaining
king. "I am the resurrection and the Life!" said one
who was greater than he. SOLOMON was wrong, and
JESUS CHRIST was right.

How many tributes CHRIST paid to the worth of life !
Would He have stood in the way of that widow's sorrow
with His "I say unto thee, young man, arise ! " if it had
been raising one up to vanity? Standing at the tomb of
His dead friend in Bethany, whom He loved, would He
have bidden "LAZARUS come forth !" to nothing more
than vanity? Never! For the sick whom He healed,
for the dead whom He restored to life, He saw better
possibilities. And ever since CHRIST lived, life is somehow sanctified for all. Motherhood is a tenderer thing,
because CHRIST was born of a woman. Brotherhood is
worthier and nobler, because CHRIST lived as our Elder
Brother. Fatherhood is more loving and sympathetic,
because CHRIST was the son of man and the son of GOD.
Cares are less perplexing, because CHRIST bore burdens.
Sin is less to be feared, because even CHRIST was tempted,
and overcame. Grief is less bitter, because "JESUS wept!"

AT THE ALTAR!

O LORD! what sacrifices can I render.
    Unless I give Thee here
A broken heart, a spirit bowed and tender,
    A faith that knows no fear!

I bow before Thine altar, lowly kneeling,
    And raise my sins to Thee ;
I know that from Thee there is no concealing ;
    For Thou canst all things see!

In mercy look, my many sins beholding,—
    In mercy look, I pray,
Upon my soul its sinfulness unfolding,
    And wipe all sin away !

O Lord ! I thank Thee that Thy love fails never,
    And while I longing wait
Give me to know that all my own endeavor
    Must fail me soon, or late ;

Give me to feel Thy love so warmly shining
    Within my hardened heart,
That all my life, as by some new divining,
    Shall into gladness start ;

Give me to sense that, broken-hearted, living
    Has henceforth something worth,—
That in my loss of sin some wondrous giving
    Sprang sudden into birth ;

Give me to see that through an humble spirit,
    Along a lowly way,
The blest shall come to that which they inherit,—
    Thine own Eternal Day!

AT THE END.

An old Italian proverb says :—"Every road leads to the world's end." It says truly. All ways of life run on to the same place—the place of graves—the end of the world.

But the end of the world is not alike for all, and we shall find it pleasant and kind or the reverse, according to the manner of our approach. With what a difference do men approach the close of life! Content and joy abide with some ; wretchedness of spirit sits heavily upon many others.

We pity the SOLOMONS, who have come nigh to the end with doubting and complaint, and only a calm religious philosophy for comfort. We are glad for the DAVIDS, who, not having grievously sinned, or having sincerely repented of their sin, can say in all the earnestness of undoubting trust—"The LORD is my shepherd ; I shall not want. He maketh me to lie down in green pastures ; He leadeth me beside the still waters. He restoreth my

soul. He leadeth me in the paths of righteousness for
His name's sake. Yea, though I walk through the val-
ley of the shadow of death I will fear no evil ; for Thou
art with me, Thy rod and Thy staff they comfort me."

Beside the way of God's leading there is more than
vanity. To such as walk in the paths of righteousness
an abiding vexation of soul never comes. The rod and
staff of the Great Shepherd are a sure comfort, to such
as find them a comfort at all. They who are led by
"the still waters" come to an end of the world that is
pleasant as the green pastures of their earlier finding,
and in which are only tender revelations of love and
care, and sweet surprises of song.

Ah ! if such were but the world's end for all ! Alas
for the many who draw nigh to theirs in fear and trem-
bling, and feel a twilight's shadows enveloping hope and
trust in gloom ! Alas for the many who are absolutely
without hope,—who have never learned the dear lesson
of trust that is so faithful in blessing,—who come nearer
and nearer to the end with indifference or recklessness,
and pass beyond affrighted and dismayed ! Happy indeed are they whose faith is fixed, whose expectations
are properly based,—to whom the end of the world is as
peace after battle, as gain after loss, as fruition perfecting
hope, as wages after toil, as reward after waiting,—whose
hearts have never a complaint, but are full of glorying,
and who go out of life as into a great joy !

HAVING AND HOLDING.

OUR title to things in this world is poor, at the best. And yet how many of us act as though a warranty deed covered all possessions—as though what we hold we have beyond any power to dispossess.

"Shrouds have no pockets," is a sermon full of pith. It strikes right at the root of selfishness. Accumulating for the mere love of it is smitten sharply by the one sentence. To accumulate for worthy purposes is right enough ; to accumulate that one may take pride and pleasure in the fancied having is quite another matter. The family must be provided for—and to that end accumulating is well. But to heap up for the love of it— to store away because it is pleasant to think one has and holds—this is not well.

"Give it to the poor" was one time a test of personal Christianity. Did the Christian stand such test? Alas ! no ; "the young man went away sorrowful, for he had exceeding great possessions." And to-day, as then, the voluntary giving up of acquired riches troubles men more than any one thing beside. "I have ; I will hold," impiously declares the rich man. "It is not my fault that want is abroad in the land. I have made my own money ; others must make theirs." So the rich man clasps his purse more closely, and congratulates himself that mortgages are not perishable property and his possessions are secure.

"I have; I will hold." Poor falsehood! How ill it will serve in the end! "I have; I must lose," would be the truer rendering, and "I will give away and so will keep," the best rendering of all. For it is only that with which we bless others that really blesses ourselves.

THE HILLS OF GOD.

'T is like a narrow valley-land,
    This earthly way of mine ;
Before me, clad in glory grand,
    I see the hills divine—
Those heights the saintly long have trod—
The Hills of Hope, the Hills of God !

Though mists of doubt enfold me in,
    Though through the dark I grope,
The upward path my feet may win
    That mounts the heavenly slope ;
And walking through this lowland here
I know the Hills of God are near.

Unto them oft I lift mine eyes,
    That oft with tears are wet,
And through the mist they calmly rise
    Where sun no more shall set.
To me forever grand and fair
The Hills of God—my Help is there !

OUR LITTLE ILLS.

THE little ills that flesh is heir to,—how they crowd into our life! How they chafe us! How they rob love of its sweetness, happiness of half its joy, sunlight of its clearest brightness, and glad content of its peace! How they tire us with dull sounds, how their endless repetitions cut deep into our very being! Ah, these little ills! When life becomes a dreary thing, and we stumble by the way, it is often not because of any great burden which we bear, but because of many little ones.

And it is strange how we will persist in taking them up needlessly,—how we search for them, as it were, and are surprised almost if perchance we find them for a time slipped off. The most serious drawback to our enjoyment is this,—that we will not be happy when we can,— that we go about continually hunting after some petty, goading thing to prick us into unrest. So when we might possess our souls in peaceful patience we are fretting and worrying all the day long, and besides being wretched ourselves are the cause of miserableness in others.

The relative heed paid to little ills is astonishing, when we come to think of it. A man will bury his wife with real Christian resignation, though he loved her fondly, who would fume about the house like a mad lion were one of the children to misplace his cane or spectacles, or did his excellent companion chance to neglect his shirt buttons.   And a good mother, fond of her children as any mother could be, will bear the death of one with noble, womanly fortitude, when to find that her thimble is missing, or that the servant has allowed a loaf of bread to burn, will set her into a high-voiced complaint fearful to listen to.

We have known very fair Christian people to fly into a violent passion because they did n't happen to agree on some little point of argument; and we have seen those whose creed was "swear not at all" get very near cursing because some thoughtless person left a door open, or trod on their toes, or said some keen, biting word on purpose to annoy.   Yet they thought themselves very exemplary, and in many respects they were.   But they were not heroes.   They never would be, though they should do some deed worthy of fame.   The Christian hero governs himself.   He bears daily vexations without wincing.   The little ills which none can avoid he laughs off, and in so doing grows the stronger to grapple with those which must be grappled.   And if there were more such we should see more smiles in the world, and the days would be glad with a brightier cheeriness.

MY MANNA.

DEAR Lord, I hunger! feed me, here,
  As Thou didst feed Thy Israel!
And let me hear The words of cheer
  That on Thy waiting servants fell!
The bread of Heaven were sweet to me;
No longer let me hungry be!

I eat of other food, and faint—
  It does not all my want supply;
My soul in plenty makes complaint,
  Is famished, and must eat or die!
Dear Lord! a little manna send,
That I be strengthened till the end!

Alas that I so long have fed
  Upon the husks of empty pride!
That of Thy sweet and living bread
  My soul its portion has denied!
Alas that thus so late I plead
My hunger and my bitter need!

Yet, Lord, Thou hearest, even late!
  Forgive the pride that would delay;
And while in weakness here I wait,
  Give me my manna by the way!
So shall I eat, and stronger be
Because my food was had of Thee!

"BY THEIR FRUITS."

"YE shall know them by their fruits," the SAVIOUR said in His wonderful sermon on the Mount. And henceforth this was to be the test of Christianity everywhere. Is it not a just one? Can there be any more reasonable judgment of aught that was intended to be useful, than that which is here implied?

"Every good tree bringeth forth good fruit;" but O, the evil trees, how thickly they are scattered about! Out in our gardens we have trees that look well,—are thrifty, luxuriant even, in their growth. Every spring they open a wealth of blossoms, and every summer or fall they are barren of all fruit. We, ourselves, are not unlike them. We show a wealth of blossoms in good intentions, purposes and promises, but these seldom mature into the rich, ripe fruit of fulfillments and performances.

A tree that blossoms and bears no fruit, is as worthless as one that does neither. Just so with our lives; they may bloom very beautiful with promises, and yet be as valueless as though never a bud of a promise had beautified them. Blossoms are sweet, in themselves, but far sweeter for that which is hidden within. They are glad prophecies of the golden harvest. Good intentions, purposes, and the like, are very pleasant things, but pleasant only because they contain a promise. If the promise fail, then are they as chaff blown lightly before the wind.

Let us be frank with ourselves, and ask how many of our blossoms become fruit. It will not do to trust that they may ripen in a season far ahead. There will be a harvest time, by-and-by: so much is certain. It may find us with never a promise realized. And then? "Every tree that bringeth not forth good fruit is hewn down, and cast into the fire." Is the answer sufficiently plain?

The season of the ingathering of grain and other products should be an impressive sermon to us. It breathes of fulfillments, on every passing breeze. Through it the voice of the year is sweetly saying,—"In the seed-time I gave you my promises; behold how they are redeemed." Let us listen to the earnest lesson. Let us nurture the blossoms of good with tender care, that the harvest of fruit may prove a bountiful one.

HUMANITY'S DANGER.

Sin is degrading, and its consequences are terribly sad. In its manifold forms it is telling fearfully against the weal of mankind. It can not be too zealously crushed out. It can not be too faithfully fought at any time and at all times.

Yet the great danger of humanity is not in sin. The most dangerous danger of all that beset the human heart is in unbelief. Sin drove the first pair out of Paradise;

sin banished Lucifer from Heaven; but there is a paradise
to-day for all who will seek it, just as surely as though
sin had never existed, and they can find Heaven just as
certainly as though no sinner had ever been expelled
therefrom.

There has been atonement for sin, and what remains is
for all to accept that atonement.   In the way of such acceptance stands unbelief.   It takes possession of all
hearts.   Secretly, or with a bold front, it dominates over
nearly all lives.   In ways subtle as varied it is spreading
its baleful influence abroad, and is seeking the overthrow
of all truth.   Preached from popular pulpits, disseminat-
ed through popular periodicals, it is gaining an establish-
ed foothold in Christian communities.

Open infidelity is not half so fatal in its effects as this
vague, subtle unbelief.   Men shrink in alarm from
atheistic denials of GOD, who dally willingly with questionings which in the end lead to something not a whit
better.   "The *fool* hath said in his heart there is no
GOD;" many accounting themselves wise have asserted
throughout life, "There is no SAVIOUR—for me," and
have finally met the fool's fate.   Sin did not work their
condemnation,—neither sin in the abstract, nor any particular sin, save the sin of unbelief.   Faithful believing
would have gained them that, the existence of which
they so unwisely denied.

"How oft would I have gathered you," was said of
those stubborn and rebellious of old.   It is a live saying
to-day.   Under the wings of protection and preservation
we may be gathered, if we will.   But will we?   Do we

so much fear an end past all hoping as to accept the kind- ly offer ? Or are we stiff-necked and obstinate in our unbelief, and do we utterly refuse all tenders of mercy because, in our short-sightedness, we may not see clear- ly just how those tenders come to us, or just what is the character of Him by whom they are made ?

LITTLE BY LITTLE.

LITTLE by little the skies grow clear ;
Little by little the sun comes near ;
Little by little the days smile out
Gladder and brighter on pain and doubt ;
Little by little the seed we sow
Into a beautiful yield will grow.

Little by little the world grows strong,
Fighting the battle of right and wrong ;
Little by little the wrong gives way,
Little by little the right has sway ;
Little by little all longing souls
Struggle up nearer the shining goals !

Little by little the good in men
Blossoms to beauty for human ken ;
Little by little the angels see
Prophecies better of good to be ;
Little by little the God of all
Lifts the world nearer His pleading call !

THAT was a golden text of the preacher's this morning —"Believe on the LORD JESUS CHRIST and thou shalt be saved."

And what the preacher said in relation to it was all worth remembering. Especially did some portions of his sermon seem pregnant with vital truth. He considered the character of this enjoined belief, and gave hints touching the same that it were well for us to think over often.

Saving belief is not a belief in fact, not belief in theology, but belief in a person. The searching question is not "On *what* have I believed?" but "On *whom* have I believed?" CHRIST has Himself declared—"But I, if I be lifted up, will draw all men unto me." It is not a creed that saves, not a doctrine, but a vital personality.

Thousands of men believe in CHRIST as a historical fact, who have yet no saving belief. Something more than this is needed. CHRIST in history is a crucified man ; CHRIST in the heart is a risen Redeemer. And it is this accepted, indwelling and personal CHRIST that saves men. He saves those who trust in Him, not those who simply acknowledge Him as one who *can* save. Acknowledgment is not enough, in the abstract ; belief is not enough, in theory. The acknnowledgment, the belief, must be practicalized in an act of absolute trust.

Soul-saving is purely a business transaction between the soul-saved and the SAVIOUR. There must be an actual transfer of the soul, the life, to the Saving One. This cannot be made as an experiment. There can be no contingent upyielding that is of any avail. Self yields itself for all time, or the transfer is of no use. If we go to CHRIST savingly, we must go with singleness of purpose, desiring nothing but to be made His forever.

Then it is a personal belief in a personal CHRIST. "And *Thou* shalt be saved," the text has it. Let us note that. "*Thou.*" Here is the promise for each. There is no restriction. It is as much for the vilest as the most moral. It holds as good for the thief on the cross as for NICODEMUS. Thank GOD that He sent His son into the world to preach so sweet a personal gospel!

BELIEF.

O DOUBTING heart! cling still to your believing!
 There is no sweeter way,
No solace that so surely soothes your grieving,
 No dearer hope, to-day;
 Nothing, when death is yours,
 That so endures.

9

All creeds of men are straws to clutch at, only,
     ⁃ When comes the final end,
And leave us cheated, at the last, and lonely,
     Without a saving friend :
     But full and firm belief
      Stops every grief.

O doubting heart ! these are not idle phrases,
     Nor pretty tricks of speech ;
Beyond our present, with its winding mazes,
     The truth in them does reach ;
     Let us accept it here,
      And prove it dear !

For prove it must we all.   There comes an ending
     To every earthliness ;
Time spares not any in its final sending
     Away from earthly press ;
     How early we must go,
      We can not know.

Then doubting heart, give doubting over, ever,
     And to your trusting cling !
For faith is better than is man's endeavor,
     And sweet reward will bring ;
     God says give Him your trust,
      And God is just !

EVERY-DAY PHILOSOPHY.

THERE are silent educators in every life. Each new experience is a teacher ; each old and familiar experience but repeats an old and familiar lesson with a new emphasis. And the intent of all this is what? To take away the superfluous in our natures ; to crush out certain inordinate desires ; to displace impatience and over-anxiety with a quiet, calm philosophy which can meet all disappointments with resignation, and which is a more sure guarantee of happiness than any outward circumstance.

More than any other influence does the Christian religion conduce to this every-day philosophy. Skepticism, in exceptional cases, may wear a peaceful, unimpassioned front, and may manifest less impatience over the daily vexations than the average Christian does ; but in the majority of instances unbelief is ever troubled at heart, is not at peace with itself, and so cannot be at peace with ordinary surroundings. Moralism may surround itself with an air of serenity, but the first storm-breath disturbs it, and all the outgrowths of its being sway to and fro like young tree-tops in a storm.

And yet greatly as a fervent Christian faith tends to give placidity to one's nature, there are many more than passable Christians who have no particle of this excellent philosophy of which we are speaking. At the least trifle they are off their balance. At a word they fret, scold, worry, fume. A disappointment sets them nearly wild. A great sorrow makes them frantic with grief. A deep wrong maddens them with pain. They are the touch-me-nots of the human family, and fly all to pieces at the slightest provocation.

Are there excuses for such? Doubtless. Nature is responsible for their unfortunate condition in a large measure. But nature can be greatly made over; one must blame one's self mainly for any lack in self-discipline. Moreover, love of CHRIST in the heart is the power which re-moulds the natural man, and which if but aided in its work will accomplish noble things. In most cases the lack of every-day philosophy arises simply through personal carelessness. Men don't try to check natural impulses. The first thought of the mind, the first promptings of the heart, are yielded to. Afterwards the penitence may be deep, even unto tears, but it brings no fruit. That is the trouble. To err and then repent of it is the daily experience of every one who fails to acquire Christian philosophy, and it is sorrowful to think that such experience, repeating its teachings. impresses no lasting lesson.

IT IS WELL.

THE air has borne some tender words,
As sweet as melodies of birds,
And benedictions soft and clear
Have trembled on the waiting ear ;
But never sweeter accents fell
Than Faith has uttered—" It is well."

Hope sits through each to day and waits
The opening of to-morrow's gates,
And Patience wearily abides
The veil that each to-morrow hides ;
But whether good or ill foretell,
Faith sweetly whispers—" It is well."

Alas for him who never hears
The words that quiet doubts and fears ;
Who, bent with burdens, plods along
With never any heart for song ;
Who murmurs, come whatever will
To bless or chasten—" It is ill !"

How dark the night when shine no stars !
How dull and heavy being's bars
When through them Faith can never see
Green fields beyond, and liberty !
How sad the day when wailing knell
Is louder than the " It is well !"

As soothing as a soothing balm,
A grand and yet a tender psalm

Is floating ever on the air,
Is blending with the mourner's prayer,
And saddest plaints that ever fell
Find answer in the " It is well!"

COMPLETENESS OF FAITH.

ONLY the other day, at the burial service of one famous the world over, a famous singer sang " I know that my Redeemer liveth." He over whose coffin the melody was breathed forth, had murmured the same words, in one of his last lucid intervals, as though they held rare comfort.

And do they not? Spoken in the completeness of faith which they really illustrate, they have all the comfort words can have. " I *know* that my Redeemer liveth." There is no doubt whatever, here. It is absolute knowledge. The "I know" covers all questioning. Others may doubt, "I *know*." Others may be in the dim darkness of unbelief; here in faith's clear sunlight "I know" and am content.

"I know that *my* Redeemer liveth." Here is the sweet individuality of the utterance, which makes it most comforting. It is *my* Redeemer that lives, not simply another's. He is as much mine, as though in all this wide world no other person lived, or had in Him an interest and a faith. That He is the Redeemer of other men I know, but my rare blessing lies in the knowledge that He is *my* Redeemer.

"I know that my Redeemer *liveth.*" That He died, we know; that He rose again we are certain; that He *lives* "I know" also, and in the knowing I am supreme-ly glad. He lives, and I may see Him by-and-by. Thank GOD that life has its variety of emphasis—that new meanings lurk under the old forms of words, that now and then we catch glimpses of clearer light and broader beauty! In the completeness of a faith which takes hold of all emphatic expression, and makes it its very own, let us go bravely on, until the knowledge of faith shall find its culmination in the knowledge of sight, and "we shall see Him as He is."

THE TWO MALEFACTORS.

WHEN CHRIST was crucified, two thieves died with Him, on the cross. In their death was a lesson for all the world. What was the lesson?

One gave up his long held faith of the Jews—gave up, with it, the sympathy of all his fellows when sympathy would have been sweet indeed—gave up his past of sin and crime—gave up himself, and died recognizing and recognized by the Son of GOD.

The other railed at CHRIST, scoffed Him, doubted Him, and died as he had lived—a wretch, with sin in his heart and reviling on his lips.

Here were two men, both of whom had been far from the SAVIOUR in life, both of whom were confessed criminals before the law, both of whom were meeting a just end at the hands of the law's executers. One came so near CHRIST, even at the very last, as to feel His touch of divine tenderness—to find joy and rest in His saving love. One, though at the SAVIOUR's very side, within sound of His voice, within sight of His forgiving treatment of those who maltreated and insulted Him, remained a doubter, continued his scoffing, and went straight to perdition.

There are others who live as did these malefactors—careless, sinning, wretched lives. They meet CHRIST as did those two, at the very gate of death. For some it is a lesson of hope that one malefactor's ending teaches. They may hold aloof from saving grace and love until the very last, and then come as near it as did he—so near as to feel it, to yield to it, to be saved by it. For some others there is a sadder lesson. They may find in their final nearness to CHRIST a nearness of judgment. They may die reviling, as he died,—unsaved, as was he. "This day shalt thou be with me in Paradise" said our SAVIOUR to one malefactor. The other heard no such tender promise addressed to himself. Wickedly he had lived; wickedly he died. And many have died in like manner. How many more will die as the fool dieth?

LOST LITTLE ONES.

I SOMETIMES look beyond the gateways golden,
    When sleep comes silently,
And there within the Saviour's arms enfolden,
    The little ones I see—
The little ones that in the glad time olden
    Were kissed by you and me.

I see no longing in their tender faces,
    Upon their dimpled cheeks
No touch of care has left its tearful traces,
    No pain for pity speaks ;
They laugh and sing in happiest of places,
    Through all the Sabbath weeks.

I wonder if amid their gleeful singing
    Perchance they ever miss
The mother's soft caress around them clinging,
    Her frequent, loving kiss ;
Or if they wait her coming for the bringing
    Of yet a sweeter bliss.

And then, when sleep has fled, and with it dreaming,
    I lie with open eyes,
And weep to find so real a thing was seeming,
    In sorrowful surprise,
Till thro' the darkness there does come a gleaming,
    From out the smiling skies.

And softly then a voice sayith to my weeping,
    " 'Twas not a dream you had,

Your little ones *are* safe within My keeping,
     So wherefore, then, be sad ? "
And o'er my heart a holy joy comes creeping,
     That makes me strangely glad.

IS THERE A SAFER TRUST ?

Now that skepticism, in so many varied forms, is as-
sailing our Christian religion, it is eminently proper for
all mankind to inquire,—Is there anything more certain
and sure in which to trust?   The wish to trust something or some power outside of and apart from itself, is
inherent in the human heart.   To throw aside all trust is
to blot out any hope in the future, and limit existence to
mere mortality.   Few will be satisfied by so doing.
Almost every individual's future, self-sketched, has in it
something beyond mortality's boundary, and is contingent upon some kind of religious belief.   That belief
which promises most certain fulfillment is the one most
earnestly desired.

And while the enemies of CHRIST seek to do away
with all faith in Him as the personal SAVIOUR of humanity, and sneer at that grand plan of salvation which has
the Crucified Son of GOD as its central figure, do they
offer any faith better and more desirable, any scheme
which shall hold a surer guarantee of redemption ?
Claiming JESUS the Nazarene to have been but the car-

penter's son, only human, though a man of exceeding
cleverness, do they present for our consideration any
mediator between the All-Father and ourselves more divine than He? Is there, in the whole range of skeptical
philosophy, any theory, promise or hope to which, turning away from GOD and the Redeemer we believe He
sent into the world, the soul can cling with more of satisfaction and peace?

These questions can not be easily answered in the
affirmative. Skepticism, trying to tear down the truest
and most vital part of Christian faith, has never offered
to build up a truer and worthier one,—has never develop-
ed any rock upon which mankind may rest with the assurance that it will prove more solid and enduring.
Skepticism, atheism, deism, infidelism, and all other
isms preaching aught beside CHRIST and Him crucified,
have as yet failed to do what the simple Christian faith
has done,—hold out a hope of eternal life and sustain
the believer through manifold afflictions until the hope
lose itself in fruition. The TOM PAINES, professing to
consider GOD a myth, and the future life a delusion, have
approached the grave in most abject fear, saying of death
—"It is all a leap in the dark." To all mankind, then,
the fact that no safer trust is offered especially commends
itself. To weak and doubting believers it should be a
source of peculiar comfort. Doubtings will come at
times; the faith will grow faint; the enemy will come in
like a flood; and for a little while unbelief will obtain
the mastery. Yet not for long, if only we remember
that unbelief yields no more cheering harvest,—that

when we give up our hopes in JESUS CHRIST we gain
nothing more steadfast and abiding,—that outside of
His blood and righteousness we find no surer prophecy
of everlasting joy. There is no clearer light for our feet
on earth than that which His gospel sheds ; no brighter
ray of promise illuminates the tomb than that His presence therein lent to it; and nowhere can we receive a
sweeter assurance of final resurrection than in His victory
over death and the grave, and His ascension to the
Father's presence.

IN SHADOW.

MY heart is dumb, to-night.
I sit beneath the shadow of affliction,
And hear no whisper of a benediction
    Upon the heavy air ;
I can not speak to God, His face is covered
By this thick cloud that o'er my life has hovered,—
    I can not breathe a prayer,—
My heart is dumb, to-night.

   ..   ..

My heart has found its speech !
I saw the shadow parting just above me,
And saw the face of Him who once didst love me—
    Who loves me even still ;
He spoke to me, so lovingly and tender
That all my doubt was lost in faith's surrender,—
    " Thine, Lord, and not my will ; "—
My heart had found its speech !

It behooves us to bear patiently with much that we could wish corrected, but much else demands righteous indignation on our part, and if it be not manifest we are recreant to our duty as Christians.

Certain forms of sin are becoming popularized, which should not be conceded the courtesy of silence. Things of little moment in themselves, but far-reaching in their influence and wide-expanding in their development, are constantly coming up, against which we should declare emphatic protest. Christian duty, more often than we seem to think, requires of us Christian speech—speech earnest with hearty indignation.

The great agent against evil is, and will be, public opinion. How is public opinion to be what it should be, if the best part of the public make no effort to purify it? If as Christians we fear possible allegations of cant, and so refrain from saying what we believe in regard to certain social phases, have we any right to cry out against popular sentiment in secret? Society is sadly tolerant of abuses and tendencies that disgrace and shame our enlightenment; has our individual Christianity done all it can to reform these?

Reformative work is individual work. It must begin with individual declarations, proceed individually, and end in the betterment of individual life. This process pu-

upon his liberty. He could resist the men of Philistia ; rifies the mass. Every Christian, then, should be a re- former. That which we believe unworthy, or degrading, we should instantly rebuke. Against that which tends to work evil, we should earnestly declare. We should, in fact, cultivate such a loathing for all sin, that we can not keep silence before it. Christian indignation has its spe- cial duty to perform, and if that performance be not fre- quently met there is something vitally wrong.

OUR SAMSONS.

Samson of old had splendid opportunities. Set apart for a noble work from his birth, and gifted with power to perform that work, he might have been the Deliverer of his people, and made for himself a history grand in- deed. But what were the facts? Relying on his own wonderful strength he dallied with sin. He made a jest of life. He set himself about nothing profoundly earn- est, and worthy his attention.

Voluntarily he put himself in his enemies' hands, con- fident that he could escape at will. In gratification of his lusts he entered Gaza, the stronghold of the Philis- tines, and went out only by taking the gates with him. Later, still following out his lustful pleasures, he tarried with Delilah, and amused himself by permitting attempts

but a woman's blandishments compassed his ruin. An overwhelming faith in his own might was the mischief underlying all. Though he broke the green withes, and the new rope, and escaped with the web woven in his hair, he fell at last, weakly, miserably.

His life and his death have their counterparts everywhere. There are men with possibilities hardly less than were SAMSON's,—with powers unlike his, yet equal to them,—whose lives are not less a miserable failure than his. Gifted, they use their gifts to no purpose praiseworthy ; strong in their own consciousness, their strength serves them for a time, but proves the veriest weakness in some unexpected moment, and they go down before the enemy of all good, and are wrecked forever.

These SAMSONS whose powers all go for naught,—what a melancholy spectacle they present ! And what is the lesson ? That we should not put ourselves in the way of temptation, fondly believing we can withstand it and come off unscathed. That we can not recline in the lap of any DELILAH of sin, however gentle its nature, with a certainty we shall not be shorn of what is our pride and glory. That gifts misapplied and perverted will bring us only bitterest reward ; and that without an earnest aim our life will darken into woe most fearful. Shall we make the lesson ours, and profit by it?

MY WILDERNESS.

WEARY and worn on the mountain-side dreary,
   Fainting, an hungered, with sadness opprest,—
Worn with long watches, with laboring weary,
   Tempted and troubled, but finding no rest;
Saviour of Men ! by the pain of Thy bearing
   Oft am I strengthened, in weakness, to-day ;
Often the thought of Thy wilderness faring
   Helps me along on my wilderness way

Bleeding and torn in the battle of being ;
   Hearing the tempter who speaks to allure ;
Saviour of Men ! in Thy merciful seeing,
   Grant that I fail not, but bravely endure !
Tempted and troubled, I know that Thou hearest
   All that my soul in temptation would say ;—
This the one thought that my loneliness cheerest—
   Saviour of Men ! Thou didst faint by the way !

Unto me Satan comes, pleasantly smiling,
   Rich in his proffers of bounty in store ;
Saviour of Men ! Thou hast known his beguiling,
   Proffers of wealth he hast made thee before.
There on the mountain-side, knowing Thy trial
   Waited before Thee—the cross, and its pain,
Thou didst deny him, and in that denial,
   Saviour of Men ! was humanity's gain !

Fainting, an hungered, the tempter beside me,
   Onward I go o'er the mountains of life ;

Saviour of Men ! let no evil detide me
   Let me not fail in the midst of the strife !
Thou who wast weary and worn with Thy faring,
   Tempted and tried on the wilderness way—
Saviour of Men !— by the pain of Thy bearing
   Strengthen me now in the strife of to-day !

MAN'S NEED.

THE desire for sympathy exists in every human heart. We all feel that we need some one to whom we can go in the fullest confidence, who will sympathize with us— who will bear a part of our burdens by becoming acquainted with them. There may be stoics—men who appear wholly indifferent to the concern of their fellows —who go about apparently giving no sympathy and asking none—but somewhere and at sometime in their lives they prove insufficient to themselves, and long for sweet and tender sympathies with the deepest longings humanity knows.

With the distrust which man naturally feels for his kind, the desire for and the real need of sympathy is seldom quite satisfied through any human agency. Friendly regard, and the affection of kindred, do much toward satisfying, it is true, but they do not always do enough. In a sense which many who read this will understand, they fall far short. Every heart has, now and then, cer-

tain vague, half-denied hopings and aspirations which
it shrinks from imparting to even the nearest and dearest.
Many have weary, sickening burdens that they never allow
human eye to look upon. Many more have convictions
of duty, questionings as to labor, doubtings as to an
hundred things in life, that cannot be properly compre-
hended by any sympathy not divine and Omniscient.

Man's need, then, is of that sympathy which only can
be found in a heart having divinity within it, and yet
possessing perfect knowledge of humanity's longings and
besetments. The Christian finds this need fully met in
the great heart of his Redeemer. If he be sorrowing,
and in deep grief, he can speak of it to the "Man of
sorrows and acquainted with grief," and be comforted.
If he be tempted, CHRIST's sympathy is complete, for He
was likewise tempted. In every contingency which
weak human nature may chance upon, the sympathy open
to the Christian is perfect, and contains a blessing.

Human sympathy, even when it is most sincere, most
freely given and most satisfying, satisfies in but a meager
way. It lacks something, we often feel, sweet as it may
be—much as it is craved. But the divine sympathy is
wonderfully full of consolation and cheer; it possesses a
power over the heart that may not be measured.—that can
be felt, but can not be described. He leads a poor life who
keeps aloof, in the main, from all sympathetic associations with his fellows; he leads a life poorer, far poorer
still, who shuns the outreaching of that Divine Heart,
whose sympathies, if received and welcomed, would hap-

pify and ennoble the hearts of all mankind. Such an one misses the great joy that might otherwise gladden his life, —goes searching through the years for what he can never find,—and comes, finally, to believe that existence is a fearfully dull, unhappy thing. His need to-day, will be his need to-morrow, because what would fill it is shut out, and what is useless only is sought after. The hunger for sympathy never can be satiated upon husks.

BY THE WAY.

A WEEPING widow walked beside the bier
    Whereon her son lay dead ;
And one who sought the city's gate drew near,
    And words of comfort said.

How swift His sympathetic soul to see
    Her deep and bitter grief !
How swift and sure as ever then was He
    To give His glad relief !

Perchance she stood in sorrowful amaze
    When first His voice she heard ;
Perchance sad wonder went before her praise,
    To hear His wondrous word.

Perchance they grew impatient at .His speech,
    The burden dear who bore ;
Perchance they marveled vainly, each with each,
    Who would the dead restore.

A stranger He? ah, yes! but one whose heart
    Went out to every woe;
In whose great love all suffering souls have part,
    Where'er they weeping go.

" I say to thee "—·O, marvelous surprise
    That in His saying spoke!—
" I say to thee, young man,"—blest word—" Arise !"
    And straight the youth awoke.

Awoke and rose from out the saddest sleep
    That mortals ever take,
O'er which we bend our bleeding hearts and weep,
    And wonder where they wake!

Awoke and walked.   And He who met him there
    Went on His lonely way,
But ever meets with the same wondrous care
    All weeping souls to-day.

Did e'er so sad a journey see an end
    So marvelously glad?
To-day the same all-wise and tender Friend
    Awaits all souls as sad.

Who goes to bury something all his own—
    Some hope his only stay—
May marvel much to hear that tender tone
    Beside the weary way.

He sought and found the city's gate who said
    " I say to thee Arise !"
But for all hearts who weep beside their dead
    He has His glad surprise !

THE GATE BEAUTIFUL.

RUTH has been reading of that poor unfortunate who used to wait at the gate that was called Beautiful, to receive alms from those who went up to the temple to worship, — the one whom the disciples blest not with silver or gold, but with the gift of bodily strength and vigor, through the name of CHRIST.

Do not we all wait at some Gate Beautiful through the years, expectant of good gifts to be doled out to us? Alms of a kind fortune we would receive, — the silver and gold of some hoped-for blessing. Perhaps it is given, but we never have enough. Every day we are carried by ambition, by hope, by greed, mayhap, to the place of passing, and there we tarry, never so fully blest that we would not go again.

Perchance we never think, as very likely the unfortunate alms-taker never thought, that there is a better blessing possible to us than the one we wait for. Perhaps we never recognize that good can come to us apart from this one line in which we are accustomed to its coming. But the better blessing is possible ; the greater good may gladden us; and from our idle waiting we may rise to a life of active work—to a being and doing so much nobler and worthier than the old that we should seem new men indeed.

All disciples may find a profitable lesson at the Gate Beautiful.   Here was a man in need.   They might have said, as they did say, "Silver and gold we have none," and considering this a sufficient excuse they might have passed on unhelping.   Yet they did not.   Though they could not do for the man according to his desire, they could do for him after all.   They improved their opportunity.   Would that all disciples of the Master were as willing as they !   All have not their power to heal ; but true discipleship carries some power with it, which may be exerted to human good.   The power to uplift, and help on, in one way or another, belongs to each of us, even if there be no pence in the purse.   We may be something better than alms-givers, if we will make use of opportunities offered.   Shall we not?

THE SUMMER IS ENDED.

"THE harvest is passed, the summer is ended."   Thus read RUTH a few minutes since, before the twilight fully deepened.

And sitting here now, the words come up again for our meditation.   The summer is ended—the summer of rest, of relaxation, of recuperation, for many ; the summer of idleness, of fashionable folly, of wickedness and dissipation for many more.   Back from the cool nooks, the quiet resting places, come those who went for their bodily good ; back from haunts of fashion and foolishness, of sin and shame, hie those who sought there only excitement and feverish waste of time.

The summer is ended. To all, what has it taught? Are any rested in spirit?—calmed by the peace of Nature and made glad by holy communion through Nature with Nature's God? Are any strengthened in their resolves to be more earnest in the work of the future—to help on God's purposes with a firm heart and an unfaltering hand? Are any (would they all were!) sick of all the glitter of gold, the shams of folly, the sins of fashionable unrest, and ready to cry out in the anguish of remorse because the summer is ended and their souls not saved?

Summer's passing should bring much of sober reflection, of serious resolves, of quickened spirituality. If there be one time more than another when man gets nearer his Maker, it surely is the summer time, when God speaks daily in the tender rustle of leaf and branch, in pleasant breezes, and by the rippling water-brooks. And whoever hears the "still, small voice" through day after day of happy idleness should return to labor profited. Whoever hears not the voice so still,—whoever listens most for speech of fashion only,—should return to autumn walks, and sigh for opportunities lost, for good ungained, and being all unblest.

BLESSED ARE THE MEEK.

THEY go forevermore unblest
Who cherish closely in their breast
The pride of earth ; all goodly things
Fly past their reach on silent wings,
And worthless is the prize they seek ;
But ever " Blessed are the meek ! "

The forms that walk erect and proud,
And trumpet their own praises loud,
Shall fall at last ; but those bowed down
Shall win at length the victor's crown,
However humble they, and weak,
For ever " Blessed are the meek ! "

God's promises are always just.
All dust of earth is only dust,
And vanishes and leaves no sign.
The lowliest is most divine,
And in its lowly being feels
A grace humility conceals.

The sweetest fragrance born of bloom
By modest mound or lowly tomb
Breathes faintly out upon the air ;
The surest answer granted prayer
Is granted unto those who seek
Believing " Blessed are the meek."

O God of love ! look down, I pray,
Upon my haughty heart to-day !

Let meekness with me e'er abide
A treasured guest, in place of pride ;
And let this truth be to me known,
That " Blessed are the meek " alone !

CHRIST IN THE HOME.

THAT story of JESUS in the little home at Bethany !
RUTH read it through again, before the twilight. While
she read, we listened. Now we think it all over, and
find a delight in thus considering what JESUS was in one
domestic circle.

There were only three of them. "And JESUS loved
MARTHA and her sister, and LAZARUS "—all three of them
—each of them. Just here comes in the best thought
about it—it was a personal, individual love which CHRIST
gave. It was not that He loved the family, as a family,
but that He loved each member of that family.

Was it only a one-sided love ? Ah, no ! MARY and
MARTHA, and LAZARUS, each loved Him. And in the
homes of to-day there may be the same reciprocity of
individual love—may be, and must be, if there is to be
in the end an individual salvation. JESUS CHRIST does
not save families. He does not in any way deal with or
do for men in the mass. He may come into a home and
love, and be loved by, one or two, or more members of
the home circle, without coming into loving, near and
tender relations to all the members.

When Lazarus died, how the weeping sisters mourned. When Christ declared that Lazarus should rise again, how blind they were. "We know that our brother shall rise again at the last day," they said. They had faith to believe that in the general resurrection He should have a part, but that Christ had power then and there to breathe new life into one long dead, they did not yet comprehend. Unto their slow comprehension Christ made a sublime revelation. "I am the resurrection and the life," said He. And to our own slow, halting trust the same declaration comes this hour.

Are any whom we love dead in sin? In Christ there may be immediate resurrection. Are we ourselves as the dead? "Whosoever believeth," said Jesus, and the "whosoever" means us. As Christ came into the little home at Bethany, loving each one there by name and in character, so He waits to enter, if He has not already entered, every home on the broad earth. For the living, His love is full of ministry. For the dead it brings a resurrection. For the living He is a Friend and a Helper, making glad with sweet affections, and sympathizing in every grief. For the dead He is a Saviour, raising up to newness of life and putting aside the dust and ashes of the grave.

There is no more touching picture of Christ than this which shows Him in the home, loving, and sympathizing, and comforting. There is none which more perfectly demonstrates His power than does this—none which more clearly sets before us an important lesson of faith. The belief that Christ can help *now*, that He can save

and restore *now*, was what those two stricken sisters needed, and it is what many need at this time. A vague,
general notion that CHRIST will help in some distant to-
morrow, possesses almost every one. A live, honest,
unshaken belief in His strength for present exigencies is
the great lack. Why should the lack exist? Why
should not this belief be universal?

HIS COMING.

" THE Bridegroom cometh !" In some night to be,
  Out of the darkness dim
This cry shall sound ; and some glad souls shall see
  The glory hid with Him !

Shall I be one of these? Or shall I lie
  Asleep in sin's embrace,
And heedless of the welcome, warning cry,
  Fail to behold His face ?

" The Bridegroom cometh !" To each waiting soul
  The cry is made to-day.
Where waves of deepest, blackest darkness roll,
  He would make light the way.

Into each life He would some glory shed,
  Some gladder blessing bring,—
To all who weep above their early dead
  A psalm of peace would sing.

" The Bridegroom cometh !"   Pause awhile and hark,
     With all-expectant ear !
For you the cry, resounding through the dark—
     The Bridegroom He is here !

DEMONIZED MANHOOD.

THE text this morning was that story of the demoniac
of Gadara, from whom CHRIST cast out the devils ; and
the preacher drew many excellent lessons from it.

That man of Gadara has many a counterpart even now.
To-day there are thousands demonized by sin—held by
its wretched power—all their better nature in complete
subjection thereto.   Sin maddens them, torments them ;
they are bruised by it ; their lives are most miserable because of its terrible presence.

How sadly true this is, we all know—some of us by
painful personal experience.   And how sweet the thought
that our SAVIOUR healed the Gadarene !   The demons
possessing the man were strong, but CHRIST was stronger
even than they.   All his life long the Gadarene had suffered from their indwelling ; now he was clothed, and in
his right mind.   There were no more roamings of the
hills by day, no more nights among the tombs, no more
bruisings.   Thenceforth he was free !

Are *we* free ?   Has any demon of sin still a lodgment
in our hearts ?   Or do we hold to one or more, even

yet? Has the Saviour come to us as He came to all those in Gadara, and are we praying Him, as they prayed Him, to depart out of our coasts? Would we beseech His departure for the same reason that they besought it —because, forsooth, in the healing of demonized souls a few swine may have suffered, and others—ours, perhaps, *may* suffer?

Verily there *are* men in the world, and their name, like that of the devils possessing him of Gadara, is legion, who think more of their swine than they do of human beings. No matter what becomes of the souls of men, so that their swine are saved. Swine or souls—is there not a choice? Ask the dram-seller, the gambler,— any whose pockets are lined with the hearts and hopes and possibilities of their fellows. What is their answer? "Souls?—what are souls to us? The bestial nature is ours; do not meddle with it. On the swinishness of those around us we fatten—hinder us not."

Among all sad facts there is not a sadder one than this,—that men should so weigh in the balance their paltry self-interest against the eternal welfare of immortal souls. And it is a fearfully significant lesson taught in the last portion of that story of the Gadarene—a leson so significant that it seems as if no lover of gains could put it lightly aside—the men of Gadara never saw again the form of Him whose presence might so richly have blessed them.

"AM I MY BROTHER'S KEEPER?"

"AM I my brother's keeper?"   As of old
   The question comes from lips of murderous Cain.
Through lustful passion, or through greed of gold,
   Is unsuspecting Abel foully slain,
And Conscience parries, with a feigned surprise,
The query where the sin of murder lies.

"Am I my brother's keeper?"   Yesternight
   A life went out in darkness and despair ;
Fiends mocked and jeered and jibbered at its flight,
   And curses left no room for breath of prayer ;
What recks the Cain who stands with visage grim
And fills the glasses to their damning brim ?

"Am I my brother's keeper?"   Day by day
   With luring smiles the weak to death are led ;
With trustful steps they walk the tempting way,--
   Their blood be on the smiling tempter's head !
O Cains ! too many die who weakly trust ;
But God lives on, and God is true and just !

Aye, God lives on !   His patience lingers long,
   His mercy through the weary years can wait ;
And Right may suffer at the hands of Wrong,
   But recompense is coming. soon or late !
"Am I my brother's keeper?"   God of Right,
Hear, Thou, and answer in Thy righteous might !

THE DIVINE HEALING.

"WILT thou be made whole?"

On a week-day evening not long ago the preacher took up these words, and now in this Sabbath twilight they come back to us, with a remembrance of the thoughts he deduced from them, and a bit of sober meditation suggested by that remembrance.

"Wilt thou be made whole?" The question implies unsoundness. And who of us is sound?—sound in moral nature? Do we not all need a physician? Are not some of us sick unto death? Though many will confess to no great burden of sin, there are few who do not feel a sense of imperfectness—a longing for some influence filling in and rounding out, and making beautiful, their lives.

What a sad array of sick souls! They look out weariedly from eyes wont to gaze upon glitter and show—they sigh in ever increasing unrest amid the follies of wealth and pride of social position. Sick unto death, some of them ; and there is only One Healer. "Wilt thou be made whole?" He questions. There is personality in the questioning. It is "Wilt *thou*?" It comes home to each one of us with as much significance as it came home to the heart of the well-nigh hopeless invalid by Bethesda's pool.

Ah, we are all by the pool of blessing, watchful for

the troubling of the waters,—desiring to step in and find
our sickness fled.   And what keeps us back?   Some of
us have been here as long as was the invalid of old beside
Bethesda, and like him, we are still unhealed.   And now
CHRIST comes to our very side, and the opportunity to be
made whole is ours beyond any human power to take it
away.   Any?   Not so.   Our own will may lose us all.
"*Wilt* thou?"   The healing is a thing of the present.
All the invalid had to do was to say "I will," and the
Divine healing found its consummation.   "Wilt *thou* be
made whole?"

> O Healer, hear my cry!
>   I would be whole, to-day!
> Pass me not waiting by,—
> Nor let me longer lie
>   Where all the sin-sick lay!
> I would be whole this hour;
> O Saviour, show Thy power!

SANCTIFYING TOIL.

BACK from his summer's vacation, our preacher had
not altogether gotten away from its atmosphere and suggestiveness. · He had been fishing, and so he chose for
his morning text those wonderful words of the Master to
some fisher-folk of Galilee—"Henceforth ye shall be
fishers of men." It was a rare scene, of course, that
sunrise hour on the Lake of Gennesaret, when the men

of nets had toiled all night in vain, and were worn out
with fruitless endeavor. A rare scene, and the carpenter's Son stood forth the rarest figure in it, as with sympathy quick and power certain he entered into the work
those fishers performed. His part in it was not large
but what results it brought! He told them where to
cast their net, and gave a miraculous draught as reward
for their obedience.

"It is a pleasant thought" says RUTH now, as we talk
it over in the twilight; "a pleasant thought, that CHRIST
sought out the very lowliest when about to commission
His disciples. Taking men from the humblest calling,
entering into the real spirit of that calling before such a
choice, He thus sanctified all effort. No wonder SIMON
PETER recognized Him there at once, as super-human,
and fell down before His divine presence."

"And yet that was a strange prayer of PETER's," some
one remarks, " 'Depart from me, for I am a sinful
man.' "

"Yes," is the answer : "because PETER was sinful, the
more need for CHRIST to tarry with him and bless him.
But SIMON was always doing wise things in an unwise
way. The Master had come here into PETER's plain every-
day life, and had wrought a miracle. Touching, so, the
man's actual, ordinary being, CHRIST's own being was
now clearly revealed. There had been another miracle
only a day or two before ; the woman sick of a fever had
been restored ; but the surprise on account of CHRIST's
power does not appear to have been so great as now.
Perhaps it is always so. Perhaps we never so thoroughly

11

understand the Master's nature as when He comes into our daily toil and shines out upon it with marvelous strength.

"And when do we need the presence of CHRIST more than, or so much as, in the daily being and doing of our lives? We toil all the night long often, and our work avails us nothing. We grow discouraged. The heart and the flesh fail us. What shall we do that we have not done? Then if happily CHRIST speak to us, as the day breaks—and it is mostly day-break when He does speak —and if we respond in ready faith which says 'Nevertheless at Thy word we will,' we shall surely find that which we seek. For if the SAVIOUR sanctified all labor, as I believe He did, He, in a sense at least, gave surety that labor shall bring its blessing. If not to-night, then to-morrow; if not on the morrow, then some near day in the By-and-By. I wonder what people did without a to-morrow that was certain before CHRIST came into the world.

"Blessed be they that work, for they shall not wait without promise! I fancy we are all disciples, somehow, and that often the Master stands by our side, when we are faint and heart-weary and utters His glad 'Henceforth.' But before that comes a 'Fear not,' and wisely too, since we grow troubled for the end so often and so soon, and are ready to give up. Is it night now where any tired soul stands? The morning is near at hand, and when it dawns our pitying LORD shall speak the one dear word of comfort."

THE EVER ABSENT.

I CAN not think her dead : I see her yet,
    Her smile a sudden glory shining through,
As if her life could never quite forget
    A gladder being that it sometime knew,
And all the memory warmed within her face
With catching glimpses of some olden grace.

Her smile — it had a radiance all its own,
    Though possibly the angels bask in such ;
And haply her sweet face had somewhere known
    The added sweetness of an angel's touch,
And this was what it ne'er forgot, the while,
But thought upon serenely in her smile.

For somewhere angels do their impress lend,
    Upon the faces that we dearest prize,—
Somewhere, sometime ; and then when comes the end,
    And those we love, despite our moaning cries,
Go outward from us where we may not see,
And leave behind them but a memory,

Methinks the angels call them fondly thence,
    To see if vestige of their touch remains,—
To see if, mid the waiting and suspense,
    The carping care, the perils and the pains.
A trace of signet holy lingers there ;
And afterwards their presence can not spare !

And so I think she went.   She heard the call,
   And said " I come," with that rare smile of hers,
Leaving the earth,—its many beauties all,
   Her pets that were her willing worshipers,
Her friends that clasped her close and prayed her stay,—
And sweetly walked along the unknown way ;

Till, seeing through the darkened way she went
   The glory of her smile so radiant shine,
The angels met her, lovingly intent,
   And led her up the wearying incline,
And finding nothing of their impress fled,
Forever choose that we should think her dead !

GOD'S LEADING.

"HE leadeth me in green pastures, and beside the still waters ! "

Blessed picture of that rest we yearn after and which seems commonly so far away ! *Does* GOD lead ? If the green pasture-land is not yet opened to our tired eyes—if the way is yet hard and stony to our wearied feet—*shall* we come out into all the comfort and restfulness of lovely fields and pleasant paths by-and-by ? So we question ; and GOD will forgive the question, and answer it in His own good time, if, though heart-sick and discouraged, we press on and fail not.

But let us not forget, meanwhile, that GOD's leading implies a willingness to be led. We can go our own way. He will not compel us. We can seek for the green fields of our hope, asking no help, relying upon no guidance. When GOD through His son said "Come unto me and I will give you rest," it was not as a command, but as an invitation, to be accepted or refused. We may refuse,—alas! how many do ! We may walk on and complain that the still waters of peace flow far beyond human finding. Yet still the placid waters do flow, and some good souls walk beside them and complain not all the day long.

GOD's leading ! It is twilight ; and yet the way never darkens. It is thick night ; and yet we stumble not.

> Tender Shepherd ! all the way,
> With Thy leading, is as day ;
> Twilight dim, or deepest night,
> Darkens not Thy watchful sight ;
> Led by Thee, my willing feet
> Soon may find Thy pastures sweet ;
> Lead me, then, by waters still,
> In Thine own Eternal will !

MEN have died poor, who all their life long revelled in wealth ; men have gone out of the world rich beyond measure, who had small earthly possessions, and all because they had given themselves away to CHRIST, and been bountifully given to of GOD's love in return.

"He that believeth shall not make haste," was the morning's text, and the preacher drew from it excellent lessons for us all.

God's ways seem very slow, sometimes. What we would see done waits long for the doing, and we grow impatient. But if we believe in God we should possess our soul in patience. In His own good time everything will come right.

Men forget, often, that the Creator still controls the world. In the midst of the anti-slavery agitation, when those who believed the slave bitterly wronged saw only darkness ahead, certain ones held a meeting, and Frederick Douglass made a speech. It was terribly earnest in behalf of his people. As he was proceeding with an appeal to all friends of freedom to rise at once in their might, and strike off every shackle, a tall, gaunt negress —Sojourner Truth by name—arose in the assemblage, and fixing her eyes searchingly upon the speaker said—

"Frederick, is God dead?"

She was a living exemplication of the truth—"He that believeth shall not make haste." And to all such God is not dead. He is a veritable Presence, and in His hands all human affairs can be trusted.

There are little things often, that trouble us, and that

render us impatient of the end. Yet GOD is as much alive to these as to those of greater magnitude. Let us trust Him, then, in these. The fret and the worry of soul concerning them, in which so many indulge, is idle. Worse than that, it is sinful, and works harm.

ALONG THE WAY.

WHOM have I, Lord, within Thy heaven but Thee?
    And there is none beside,
    On all the earth so wide,
That can to me both Friend and Helper be.
    Forsake me not, I pray,
    Throughout the lonely way,
But kindly walk my dubious path with me!

Of old Thou wast the present Helper, Friend,
    Of holy men who trod
    Appointed ways of God;
To me Thy gracious presence henceforth lend,
    Though I have sinned so sore;
    Nor leave me evermore,
But cheer and comfort grant me till the end!

Thy son, our own dear Elder Brother, came,
    And sorrowed, suffered, bled,
    For us His life-blood shed,
And died at last a death of deepest shame.
    Now for His sake I cry;
    Nor canst Thou e'er deny
The prayer put up to Thee in His dear name!

Then hear me, Lord, I pray, and let me know
That Thou, indeed, hast heard
My every prayerful word,
By going with me wheresoe'er I go!
No way with Thee is dark ;
And with Thee I shall hark
For speech of Thine, so tender, sweet and low.

Amid the noises jarring on my ear,
So full of fret and pain,
So vexing and so vain,
Thy still, small voice I fain would ever hear!
Speak to me, day by day,
Along the troublous way,
So shall I know that Thou art always near !

THE POVERTY OF RICHES.

" For riches take wings and fly away."

Was Ruth reading, or syllabling her own thought,
when she uttered these words? We could not tell.
Finally, after a little pause, she said :

"Yesterday I read an account of the late panic in
Wall street, and it seemed very sad. Some men were
rich in the morning, and at night had not a dollar.
What a sudden change for such ! It must be hard to
feel so poor after enjoying wealth."

Then we were silent a while, and full of thought. At

last one of us—was it the home-heart, from her easy-chair?—broke the silence again.

"Yet is there poverty even in riches."

Ah, yes! Poorest of all GOD's poor are many who own houses and land, and know no earthly want. GOD's poor? Nay; for the poor of GOD have an abundance that fails not. Of their wealth the rich know nothing. Their treasure is safe. Banks may break, but they are secure. Public confidence may falter, they have no fear. For GOD's poor was it spoken—"Blessed are the poor, in spirit."

Souls may suffer while bodies roll in luxury. The poverty of riches is beyond all common cure. Millions for the signifying,—but no real joy. Carriages and diamonds,—but no peace. Mortgages and coupons,—but no enduring comfort. Poverty! It is hard to go an-hungered; it is hard to feel pinched and hemmed in; it is hard to want beautiful things,—to long for much and have little; it is hard to go on and on amid deprivation and care, and know no satisfying of the merely human needs. Ah, yes! But is it not harder to hunger for what no money can buy?—to go forever athirst?—to long for something which shall fill the heart full, and make the whole being glad? Verily it is. They are not always rich who seem blessed of Plenty. They are not always poor who want.

THROUGH the twilight silence we have spoken no word. What each has been thinking of, who shall say? It is RUTH who, as usual, is first to speak.

"It is hard to be thankful amid want, and distress, and great discouragements. I wonder how many will feel on next Thanksgiving Day that it is simply impossible?"

RUTH is always wondering about the *hard* things of life. Well, so are many others. The hard things are plenty, and there is always enough to wonder over.

"It is easy, now, for us, to offer thanks. We feel very grateful to GOD for His goodness unto us. But I have seen people who thought GOD not very good to them, and I could'nt help feeling that I might think just so, too, if I were in their place."

We ponder awile upon RUTH's words. Are there, then, some who seem neglected of GOD? Is it indeed true that to any soul GOD is not good? Beyond question there are many not good to themselves. They sin, and find joy in sinning; they forget the Maker's claims and remember only self; they in no proper degree recognize GOD and live for Him. That GOD withdraws His blessings from such is but natural. That they often abide in want, and lack much, is not strange. That they distrust

supreme goodness, and are devoid of all gratitude, is but
the logic of their course and character.

Gratitude is the child of faith and love. Our thank-
offerings measure the love we enjoy. Do we love any
one much? Then we are grateful for small favors extend-
ed by them. There is great danger, it is true, that we
come to take every gift as but our due, and so receive
whatever is tendered with indifference and ingratitude.
It is just here that we sin most. GOD is our father, we admit, and He is bound to mete out according to each
necessity. But we err. His fatherhood does not bind
Him for our needs. Life itself was His free gift. Every added pleasure, or benefit, or help, is likewise a free gift,
and in no degree whatever ours by right. For the small-
est favor granted we stand debtor.

And there are none who go on through the years unhelped. The poorest pauper of all has been given of
GOD. In some manner he does not heed, GOD has cared
for him. In some way he does not suspect, GOD is doing
for him. The very fact that he is a pauper does not establish anything against GOD. The gift of life was his ;
he might have made of it all that another did make of a
gift similar. Why he failed is not for any to say. GOD
knows. GOD permitted the failure, though He did not
cause it. GOD is not Fate, and for this let us ever be
thankful.

For all that we *may* be, let us thank Him to whom we
are indebted for the possibility. We may never attain to
it. We may go through the years poor in possessions,
lean in soul, and never satisfied ; yet for the possibilities

we are debtor. It is better to praise God for the Might Have Been, than sigh over it. It is better to see in what is, a hope, than always to complain because it is not a fulfillment. God gives the hope, and we make our own fulfillment.

Ruth doubts this, and says there are persons, of the very best intentions, whose endeavors have been well put forth, who nevertheless have failed, and see no occasion to thank God for failure.

True, but even these may feel glad that it is no worse. Very few get to the lowest deep of want and failure. Then again, one should be thankful for others' joy and success. Is there not a selfishness of gratitude? To give thanks only for what is received in person is most meager thanksgiving indeed. In the great world, one is a little atom of a great mass. If the thousands are blest, let us rejoice, though we sit in poverty of being forevermore.

THANKSGIVING.

Some days of sweet content are mine ;
    Some days of waiting sore
For joys I can but half divine,
    So far they go before ;
Some days of doubt, some days of cheer,
    Some days so sweet and strong
They bear me on an atmosphere
    Of trusting faith along,

Till on the mountain-tops I stand
And view the welcome Promised Land!

And for these days my thanks are due—
 Accept them, gracious Lord !
For all these days, of every hue,
 That with my life accord.
Each day within it holds a good
 Of some diviner kind
Than any, dimly understood,
 My consciousness can find,
And for the good I can not see
My thanks go out, O Lord, to Thee !

I know that all about my life
 Some unseen blessings wait,—
That through the deafening din of strife
 Some sweet songs palpitate ;
That God is good, howe'er it seems,
 And doing richly worth ;
That in the brightest sunlight beams
 His angels visit earth,
And in the shadows walk they still,
Fulfilling His own holy will !

For all I am my thanks I give ;
 For all that I might be !
The life is mine I do not live—
 My gift, O God, from Thee !
I thank Thee for its brighter days
 That some time I may know,
And ask Thy guidance through the ways
 That to it haply go ;
And so with thanks for blessings mine
I wait the leading all divine !

"Blessed is he whosoever shall not be offended in me."

This was the preacher's text to-day. Christ spoke the words in partial answer to that doubt of John the Baptist which sent his disciples to the Saviour to ask of Him concerning His identity.

Ever since John's time there have been doubters, even among those who believe most in Christ. It is natural that men who have accepted Him should sometimes feel their faith shaken. Because Christ's ways are not our ways. This was what troubled John. Jesus came not as John had expected Him to come. The manner of His administration was hardly that of a kingly Messiah. In everything, this One whose coming John had preached was in marked contrast to the ideal previously conceived.

And so it is with us. We conceive of a Saviour who shall appear thus and thus—who shall deal with us after our own peculiar notions of justice and expediency—who shall help us through certain agencies with which we are familiar. We accept the Saviour, and behold we are grievously disappointed, for He is far different from our conception of Him. His dealings with us are not at all as we desired, and do not accord with our views of justice and expediency—the ministering agents He employs suit us not. So we are offended in Him. Misgivings enter into our minds, and we cry out distrustfully, "Is this the CHRIST ?"

There is hardly a sweeter beatitude in the Sermon on the Mount than this text of the preacher's. It means much for us all. Blessed is he who murmurs not though he be smitten ; blessed are they who accept all divine dealings as wisest and best ; blessed are such as be not impatient under long withholding ; blessed are all whose will is humbled, whose pride has frequent fallings, whose life is unsatisfying, yet who give not over to doubt and despair : it is as though CHRIST had said all this in detail, and very much more.

There was ever a mine of meaning in the speech of JESUS. Men have thought upon single sentences of His until they became part and parcel of their beings, growing more and more fruitful as these broadened towards completed growth. And this blessing—has it not special significance for us all ? Are we never offended in CHRIST? Do we never question when sudden affliction smites, or coveted wishes fail of fulfillment, "Is this He ?"

How meager ours are, often ! We take so much that comes to us of good and comfort as a matter of course ! Perhaps we do not really feel, but we seem to, that GOD only does His duty by us at the best—that He is bound to provide for us all that is provided ; and some will even complain because His provision is not more full and satisfactory.

Sitting here now, in the firelight, thinking of the Thanksgiving so soon to come—a day which will be to so many fuller of feasting than of thanks—we call to mind the words of a preacher to whom we often listened in the years gone by, who had a way of putting things very striking. It was in a prayer and conference meeting, of an evening like this, when thankfulness seemed to be most the subject of thought. and one gentleman had remarked upon his own lack of gratitude to GOD for mercies enjoyed. The time for closing the meeting had come, as he sat down, and eccentric Dr. M— closed it in a way we shall never forget.

"That is always the fact," said he, as he leaned back meditatively in his chair, "ingratitude is our greatest sin." Then, his face lightening up as it was wont when a new conceit flashed upon him, he continued—"We are not half thankful enough for the blessings we receive, and so we don't receive half as much as we might, often. You take a little pitcher to the well, and you get your little pitcher full. You take a great pail to the well, and you get your great pail full. But you mus'n't expect to carry a little pitcher of gratitude to GOD, and take away a great pail full of blessing !" And, rising suddenly, he said, in his abrupt way "'Take that and go home !" and this was our benediction.

The little pitcher of gratitude—how many carry it ! It is borne in our prayers daily, perhaps—prayers that only dimly recognize GOD's goodness, and have little of real heart-thankfulness within them. And shall we carry only the little pitcher in days to come, especially in that day which is set apart for one great thank-offering of the people ? He who gives us all things deserves better of us all. What comes to us comes *not* as a matter of course. It is a free gift. Let us fill our largest vessels full of gratitude, and mayhap we may carry them away from GOD's altar overflowing with blessing.

IN THANKFULNESS.

I FOLD my hands in idleness, to-day ;
  My heart is yielding its thank-offering.
"Of little worth am I, O Lord !" I say ;
  "And little can I to Thine altar bring,

But that I fain would give to Thee always ; "
And in my heart I chant a psalm of praise.

I backward look upon my life, and see,
   Above it. through the years, a Presence bent,
And know what came, of good or ill to me,
   Was by that Presence in all kindness sent ;
And if some joys I want, in thankfulness
My heart goes out for those I do possess.

The skies above me wear a sunny smile ;
   The clouds may come—it will not wholly fade ;
And sunshine creeps into my life, the while,
   With warmth such as but it and love e'er made.
My finer being feels a thrill divine
As on my way the pleasant sunbeams shine.

There may have been some cherished blessings lost—
   I may have felt some momentary pain ;
My will, by God's, may often have been crossed ;
   But losing much has only been my gain ;—
And thankful for the lost, as for the won,
I fold my hands and say " Thy will be done ! "

To-day is mine.   To-day is very broad ;
   It has the fullness of the Infinite.
It reaches from my narrow life to God,
   And holds within it a supreme delight.
It has the work, and partly the reward—
The rest will come to-morrow, praise the Lord !

OUR HEART-OFFERING.

"GIVE thanks unto the LORD for He is good."

Thus read RUTH, on Thanksgiving evening. Something in her voice touched the words with a meaning new and sweet.

"For He is *good*," she repeated. "How many who have to-day listened to those words, really emphasized them in their hearts?"

We all fell to thinking. In the hush that followed, our hearts sent up anew an offering of thanks. GOD's goodness was growing in our sight.

"For His mercy endureth forever," RUTH chanted softly.

His mercy! From the heart of the great world at large should go up to GOD an offering of thanks for His *mercies*. If GOD were good alone, and not merciful, sad would it be for many. Because GOD is good and merciful both, let us rejoice.

"I read, once," said RUTH, after a little, "of a minister whose child died. At the grave, when clods had fallen heavily upon the coffin where beauty and love lay buried, the father spoke. 'My friends,' said he, 'it has been my lot to stand by the graves of many whom you loved and mourned. In your sorrow I have told you of GOD's goodness and tender mercy, and you may have thought me wrong. In your grief you may have thought

me mistaken.   But now, standing here by the grave of
my own loved one, I can say to you that all I have ever
spoken about God's goodness and mercy is true.   God *is*
good, and loving, and kind.'   I wonder if all mourning
hearts have felt like this to-day ?" Ruth queried.

And we thought of the dear friends who miss so much
from their life—of one loving woman who is companion-
less on a journey which two began together—and with
our thank-offering went up a prayer for suffering souls.
In the twilight's silence, from the corner where the
mother-heart sits, a tremulous voice breathed out a
word of comfort so tenderly that we could have wished
every mourner to hear :

"Like as a father pitieth his children, so the Lord
pitieth them that fear Him."

A CHRISTIAN HABIT

The very habit of godly life helps to keep one from
temptation and sin.   There are times, perhaps, when
spirituality is at a low ebb in the heart, and little of God's
sweet love seems to have place therein.   Then this habit
of correct living—a habit acquired through years of
watchful prayer and persistent purpose—holds the man to
circumspectness, and keeps him from many things that
might soil his soul.

As a saving feature the habit may be little worth, but

as a strong cord, holding evil tendencies in check, its value is very great. Satan rarely tempts with his wickedest pleasures, those who go straight on in their daily life, upheld by a habit strong and strengthening. He dallies with such as are uncertain of themselves, being the creatures of their own impulsive promptings, and swayed hither and thither by the power of their own passions. Passion habitually held in check, is never harmful ; but let it now and then rise to the mastery and all safety is gone by.

For safety lies only in a correct *habit*, not in an intention to be correct in the main, but to grant self certain indulgences as inclination may prompt. Just here is where sad mistakes are made. Young and old alike make them. Men are continually saying to themselves — "This indulgence will not work me harm. My life shall be mainly correct ; my self-discipline shall be rigorously maintained, with some slight exceptions ; I will abide by what my conscience dictates as a rule ; but every rule has its exceptions." And yet there *are* rules of being and doing which ought to have no exceptions—which can not admit of exceptions without absolute danger.

It is the exceptional lapses from Christian circumspectness that impair the Christian character, and weaken the Christian faith. If not too often occurring, their influence may not be so readily discovered, but it is not the less an influence, and it is not the less an influence for the bad. In essential quality it is precisely the same as though it were more plainly marked but its degree is

not so great.   Occasional sinnings may not utterly warp
the nature over, but they leave their impress, and it may
never be quite eradicated.   If the habit of life wholly
forbid these, how much better in the end. —how much
better even now !   We do not argue for perfectionism,
for we believe men will always fall far short sf sinless
living ; but we argue for a complete shutting out of the
grosser sins that lure so many to final ruin through occasional yieldings.   Nothing short of divne grace, and a
rule of life which will admit no exceptings, can save men
from these.

THE STAR DIVINE.

I sit beside my window here,
And through the winter atmosphere
I see the hills of evening rise
Against the fading sunset skies.

As one by one the stars outshine,
I think how in this heart of mine
When darkness comes, through fear and doubt,
The star of love shines clearly out.

It brighter still and brighter glows,
As deeper night my being knows,
'And looking steadfast on its ray
I half forget the vanished day.

O Star of Love divine, so blest,
Shine on forever in my breast,
That never night may come to me
So dark I can no comfort see !

The clouds are often o'er my way
So dense I walk in twilight gray,
But in thy light, O star divine,
I see my Master's face outshine !

And seeing this I walk along,
Upon my lips a grateful song ;
Within my heart a grateful prayer
That God will make all shadows fair.

Then Faith contends He ever will,
And Faith recites with tender thrill
That for a moment dims my sight—
"At evening-time let there be light !"

You have heard of the man who, when he ate a cherry, always put his spectacles on, that it might seem the larger to him ? It were better, seemingly, in some such way to magnify our hope, than continually to depreciate it. It is possible for such depreciation to work a serious harm. We think it often does. These men with small hopes seem shrunken in their Christian growth, and they actually are shrunken. It is better, vastly better, to cherish and nourish a hope, than to starve it.

NEWNESS OF LIFE.

WHAT does newness of life mean? A new life must be antedated by a new birth: so much we know. A new birth is a being born into new things, and a new life is a continuance therein. Then, as Christians, have we always newness of life? Do we continually walk in the way entered upon when the old things of sin and debasing worldliness were renounced? Or is there daily a lapsing away into habits that hurt, and indulgences that tell sadly against our soul's present and future well-being?

We may not argue that Christian living becomes old, and that therefore newness of life is impossible to one past his early Christian experience. All Christian feeling and desire is renewed day by day. it is fresh with every morning's freshness. New things are opening up to the Christian's recognition constantly—new things in the line of God's goodness and human want, of the Creator's marvelous bounty and the creature's capacity to receive and be blest. All that is great and glorious in nature, all that is sweet and tender in revelation and experimental knowledge, is baptized anew with divine grace so often that it can not become stale.

The soul has its longings and its answers, and in these is newness of life yet further exemplified. What we live upon to-day will not sustain us to-morrow. The same in kind may satisfy, yet it is different in fact. It is some-how changed. That which we pray for to-day and re-ceive, we may pray for next week, and again receive, yet it is not the same; it is new, it meets our want, it helps us on. GOD pity those to whom nothing fresh comes,—whose being is but an existence,—whose one complaint is that all things have become old !

There are some such, who claim the Christian's title, who walk in Christian fellowship with their compeers. Theirs is the old life, over and over again—the week-day routine, the Sabbath church-going. New things made their hearts glad once, but there is no longer anything new. They pray the same prayers, they feel the same faint aspirations, they cling to the same weak faith, as in earlier years. How meager it all is ! New life is new faith, new aspirations, new askings. May this newness of life make us all to rejoice !

"*JESUS WEPT.*"

CHRIST's humanity is touchingly pictured in the two words which comprise the shortest verse in the Bible. In the same chapter wherein is found the sublime declara-tion—" I am the resurrection and the life," it is recorded, "*Jesus wept.*" Divinity speaks forth in the declaration ; humanity sorrowfully manifests itself in the brief, simple record.

Though, as we read the Gospel narrations, we can readily believe the SAVIOUR to be "a man of sorrows and acquainted with grief," we never realize how closely His nature is allied to our own until we see Him weeping in sympathy with others over a friend dead.   CHRIST healing the sick, making the blind to see, causing the lame to walk, and performing all those GOD-like miracles which so clearly prove His superior power, wins our most devout worship; CHRIST sorrowing as we sorrow, stricken in heart with a grief so common to us all, calls out our deepest and warmest love.

Human grief is so very human that it moves us with a strange control.   We cannot look upon it in idle indifference.   Griefs are of many kinds, however, and not all move us alike.   Sorrow born of death has the strongest influence.   Speaking of this sorrow one said once, in our hearing,—"When a friend dies it is not so much that one we loved is dead, but that a part of our life is wanting."   And so when we see stricken ones mourning over the part of their life which they miss, our hearts respond in sincere sympathy.   When the Redeemer weeps over Jerusalem, because of its wickedness, we are touched, but in only a slight degree ; when, with MARY and MARTHA, He weeps over the dead friend and brother, we can scarcely do other than add our tears to His.

Perhaps in no other portion of the inspired narrative is the marvelous union of the divine and the human, in the person of CHRIST, so clearly shown as in this eleventh chapter of JOHN.   JESUS wept not as we weep when those we love are taken from us.   His humanity asserted itself for a moment, but had He not said to the sorrowing MARTHA—"Thy brother shall rise again?" What need that He should be long troubled in spirit? Only a moment láter, and He could say "LAZARUS, come forth," and the tomb would yield up its dead. Blending with the tears of the man was the wonderful power of the All-Father, which should bring joy to the bereaved but believing sisters, and faith to the doubting Jews.

And still CHRIST is troubled in spirit because of humanity's griefs ; still He is saying to all—"I am the resurrection and the life ;" still is the human in His nature reaching out to human natures everywhere, to draw them up towards the divine. We do not realize this enough. We think of CHRIST too much as one who was crucified for our sakes, but having been crucified is forevermore disassociated from us, and from everything allied to humanity. We need to appreciate more clearly that He is still our elder brother,—sympathizing with us, sorrowing with us, and even interceding for us.

MY THANKFUL THOUGHT.

THE Master on the Mountain, the disciples on the sea !
I sit within the twilight, and a picture comes to me—
A vessel tempest-driven, tossed in anger by the wave ;
A company despairing, seeing none to help and save ;
A lonely watcher praying on the lonely mountain side,
The entrance-door to Heaven by His prayers thrown open wide !

And now the thought of thankfulness supreme above the rest
That surge and swell for utterance within my thankful breast,
Is this: that though the waters rage, and though the tempest sweep
Around me as I sail along, or waking or asleep,
The Master on the mountain waits and He will come to me,
As I shall need Him, walking as of old, upon the sea !

There is so much to thank Him for who gave so much to each,
That my poor heart is oftentimes too full of thanks for speech,
And so I sit in silence oft, and make no sound or sign,
And yet I think my silence our dear Master can divine,
Who waits upon the mountain as He waited there of old,
Whose arms from every danger His disciples will enfold.

But now I am not silent, though my speech is faint and low,
Because a flood of feeling fairly makes the tears to flow ;
Yet through my silence only speaks this thankful thought su-
    preme—
That in my peril and my pain, when skies the darkest seem,
My life ahall know its blessedness, my being find its cheer,
My heart grow warm with gladness, in the Master's coming near !

O Master on the mountain ! surely heaven's door did ope
To prayer of Thine ingoing, and, outcoming, our great Hope !
The entrance into heaven is our gateway out of sin,
Beyond its shining portal shall the Perfect Peace begin,
But here amid the striving, 'mid the storm and tempest sore,
A hint of heaven's holding shall Thy coming bring before !

THE CHRIST-CHILD.

IT has been said that no other religion than the Christian ever had a child in it; and the fact as stated is not more curious than significant. That JESUS CHRIST came into the world as a little child, means much for us all. He began His humanity at the very beginning. Therefore there is not an experience He can not understand, not one with which He can not sympathize most keenly. And is not the fact of such near and complete sympathy most blessed to us?

Then as He came to us as a little child, like little children must we go to Him. Manhood is hardened and unyielding; childhood is trustful and yields readily. Manhood is full of doubts and questioning; childhood is trustful and questions not. Manhood stands upon rights; childhood claims none, but is willing to receive and be glad. And so we must be pliable, trustful, willing to receive CHRIST's rare blessing undoubting, if we would receive it at all.

CHRIST came so very near humanity in His earth-life, that it should be an easy thing for us to come very near Him in return. Yet it is harder than we might imagine; and it is hard simply because we insist upon holding our manhood and womanhood, our foolish lessons of the years. "Are we not men and women?" we ask ourselves, ''shall we not maintain our manly dignity and womanly reserve? Must we sacrifice individuality to win CHRIST?"

O miserable questioning! How much better is the wise trust of the child! The trusting has its reward; the questioning never. The peace of salvation never was born of questions, but of faith and prayer. It is not a product of the intellect; it springs up, and grows, and bears fruit deep in the heart. The wisest may question and find no answer; the weakest may trust and be answered to the uttermost. And all because on a morning years ago, in Bethlehem of Judea, a *babe* was born whose name was JESUS CHRIST.

THE LAND OF MOAB.

THE theme of the morning was RUTH'S Choice.

What sweeter narrative is there, in all the Bible, than this of RUTH? Here were three women—NAOMI and her two daughters, ORPAH and RUTH. The first had determined upon a return to the kingdom of Israel; and would these go also? Many years had NAOMI been in Moab, but the special tie which had bound her there was severed; she longed with an inexpressible longing for rest in old age among the people of GOD.

They had come with her, these two women, some dis-

tance on her journey. Now they must stop, or go with
her altogether. Which should it be? Should they continue on, or go back? On the one hand was Moab,
with its pleasures, its prosperity, its associations, its bright
promises for the future; over against it was Judah, des-
olate, lonely, with no prospect of worldly gain or joy.
It was heathendom and its offerings, or the kingdom of
the living GOD without these. Which?

ORPAH chose to go back. The shining hills of Moab
held more for her than Judah could hold. But RUTH?
She, too, was tempted. It may not have been easier for
her to forsake Moab than for ORPAH. She may have
been as strongly attached to its associations, as was her
sister. Yet her choice was the wiser choice, and through
these hundreds of years its sweet language has been read
and sung by Christian humanity the world over—"Entreat
me not to leave thee, or to return from following after
thee: for whither thou goest I will go; and where thou
lodgest, I will lodge: thy people shall be my people,
and thy GOD my GOD; where thou diest, will I die, and
there will I be buried."

And to-day some of us have come, as RUTH and OR-
PAH came, to the parting of the ways. Friends whom we
love we have followed to the very edge of Moab's Land.
As with those two girls, so with us,—a choice must be
made. Shall we stay in Moab? It holds for us all that
it held for them—social joys, worldly advancement, ease
and pleasure; it lures us with all the beauty of its shining
hills, and all the sweet grace of its many charms. Over
yonder is the sacrifice, the discomfort, the loneliness, the

unpleasantness, of Judah.   It is life for self, where self
may find its greatest gains ; or life for GOD, where there
may be only the gain of GOD's favor and eternal rest.

Shall we choose as RUTH chose?   Why should we not?
Often has it been proven that Moab can not satisfy till the
end.   Why prove it yet again ?

THE BLESSED THOUSAND YEARS.

WE wait the Blessed Thousand Years !
The present with its hopes and fears,
Its longings all unsatisfied,
Looks through the portal opening wide
To let the Future in, and waits
Its coming through the portal-gates.

O Future ! near and yet so far—
Where shines the bright millenial star—
Haste thy approach !   The days are long
Till Right shall triumph over wrong,
Till Morn shall chase away the Night,
And faith be verified in sight !

We wait the Blessed Thousand Years !
Dim, undefined, as through our tears
We forward look, there seems to rise
A newer earth, with brighter skies
Than those which beam erewhile on this,
Where hope attains to fullest bliss ;

Where all the fret, the din and moil,
That round these weary days of toil,
Shall find completest recompense ;
Where, unrestrained, our soul and sense
Shall feed and ripen on the food
Gleaned from the fields of perfect good ;

Where every pampered lust shall be
Unknown and man be fully free ;
Where buds of promise know no blight,
And pure desire brings pure delight ;
Where all discordant noises cease,
And only echo songs of peace !

Blest Thousand Years !   O righteous God,
The thorny paths the world has trod
Are wearying its heart and strength—
Methinks they weary Thee, at length !
Bring, then, the paths that lead erewhile
Through blooms which hide no secret guile !

We wait the Blessed Thousand Years !
We wait and labor.   He who hears
A people's prayer for nobler things,
Will give the good time swifter things :
While that for which we long and wait
Our faith and works may ante-date !

13

POWER OF PRAYER.

THE preacher's theme this morning was a common one. We have all thought more or less of the power of prayer ; we have all heard much in regard to it. Yet the morning's discourse presented one or two points in a comparatively new light, and these are just the points upon which many stumble and doubt.

GOD is not a GOD of uncertainties. His purposes are not yielding and pliable, so as to be changed by this one's request, or that one's pleading. "Then why pray?" asks some one. "If GOD's designs are already determined, why waste breath in prayer?" Because prayer is a part of GOD's plan. It is ordained in the divine economy that petition shall prelude bestowal. Anything worth having is worth asking for, is the common rule.

Prayer is spirit-born, God-willed. It is the human want, grafted on to the divine purpose. "Ask and you will receive," is the promise. It is not, however, a miscellaneous promise, made without any limitation. There are many things which we have no right to ask for—the granting of which would work us harm rather than good. It is only as touching those things the granting of which is predetermined, that the promise holds secure.

For what, then, shall we ask? Can we ever know that

we ask aright? The Holy Spirit moves to right asking ;
if we have that as an indwelling presence we shall seldom
err. There are certain vague, restless stirrings of the
soul, when a sense of personal need presses upon us as a
burden. In times like these we are moved to prayer, and
our prayer is available. Petitions of the lips are wasted
words ; the prayer of the heart, inspired by the spirit of
God, is a certain power.

ABILITY TO GIVE.

It is the time of giving gifts. Has not this season a
deeper significance than we are accustomed to think
upon ?

Life, primarily a free and splendid gift to us, was
meant to be, secondarily, a benefit to men at large. Is
the meaning fulfilled ? How much of the wealth of
being do we give to those about us ?

"But I am very poor," says one. "I am not rich in
anything which the world needs. Others can bestow of
their endowments, or of what they have acquired, but I
must be only a recipient. I have nothing to give."

So might those disciples have talked, who chanced upon that helpless man who waited by the Gate Beautiful.
They had no money, and he was there for alms. They
might have made a seemingly reasonable excuse, and left

him unhelped.   They might have said to him "We, too, are penniless;" and he would not have expected a farthing.

"Silver and gold we have none," they declared, "but such as we have give we unto thee.   In the name of JESUS CHRIST of Nazareth rise up and walk."   Was not their gift of the very best and most valuable?   And having it in their power to bestow so generously, would any excuse suffice for them to withhold the bestowing?

"*Such as we have*"—herein lies the secret of it all.   In our poverty we have yet something which some wayfarer needs.   At many a Gate Beautiful lies a waiting one, whose life we may make glad.

Weak, are we, and unable to work effectively in and of ourselves?   So were those disciples.   But there is a hint for us in their declarative command.   "In the name of JESUS CHRIST of Nazareth," they did what they did, and gave what they gave.   In CHRIST's name we also must work and give.   If, as real disciples, we stand at the Gate Beautiful, we shall fail not in giving, for the spirit will be ours, and to us will be given the means.   Are we daily passing by the waiting souls?   Then a truer discipleship is needed.   Are we all our life long withholding what men want, in mistakenness or selfish greed?   Then, by-and-by, from us will be taken that which we have, and it shall be given to him who hath not.

GOD'S TIME.

THE sun goes down, and the light fades out—
    " God has forgotten the world ! "
Over the heavens come dark and doubt—
    " God has forgotten the world ! "

The darkness deepens—in gloom we grope—
    " God has forgotten the world ! "
Hidden forever the stars of hope—
    " God has forgotten the world ! "

But see ! there's a gleam in the midnight sky !
    " God will remember the world ! "
Stars do shine in the By-and-By—
    " God will remember the world ! "

And see ! there's a glow on the eastern hills !
    " God will remember the world ! "
The glad day dawns when the good God wills ! "
    " God will remember the world ! "

Ruin and death are abroad to-day—
    God has gone out of the world !
What does it profit to preach and pray ?
    God has gone out of the world !

Truth is futile, and Right is weak—
    God has gone out of the world !
Vainly we listen to hear Him speak—
    Has He forgotten the world ?

No! He liveth, He heeds, He hears !
　　God is alive in the world !
Faith can see Him through pain and tears—
　　God is alive in the world !

He will help in His own good time—
　　God is alive in the world !
Right shall win in a day sublime—
　　God *lvies on* in the world !

GOOD GIFTS.

" If ye, then, being evil, know how to give good gifts unto your children, how much more shall your Heavenly Father give good things to them that ask Him."　Thus did RUTH repeat the text of the morning.

At every hearthstone, in this holiday time, some token is given and received, telling of kindly regard and affection.　Parents remember their loved ones; the parents in return are remembered.　All this giving of gifts is beautiful and works out a benefit.　Apart from the added nearness it imparts to domestic life—setting aside its salutary influences in the way of strengthening family ties—it is most beneficial.

Who so receives a testimonal will, if he be studious of himself, consider how little he has merited it, how much his life and thought and companionship should be improved, to be worthy of such regardful manifestation. And in the gift there is an incentive to better motive, purer action, ambition higher and nobler. With the gift's abiding abides the incentive influence, and while it abides the being grows nearer what it should be. Good gifts, to thoughtful souls, have in them more than the world sees, more than the donors apprehend.

GOD cares not for the race simply as a race, not for humanity simply as humanity, but for each individual as His own child.

"How much more!" You are tenderly considerate of your own ; you would not insult your little one's undoubting faith by putting a stone in the stocking expectantly hung ; how much more careful for His own is your Heavenly Father, than any earthly parent can be ! We may never fathom the "much more." It covers breadths we can not span, it sweeps vastness we can not look across. It comprehends the difference between the finite and the Infinite. GOD ministers to the individual want. His love and care are all embracing, yet they distinguish as individually as any human love and care can distinguish— yea, "how much more!" But the gifts must be asked for. Things come that are not asked for, perhaps, but rarely the things we need most. When they do come unasked, they are as the exceptional surprises of the holiday time. All that our being daily requires should be sought for in daily asking. All the good gifts of everyday being and doing—the loving spirit, the patience, the trust, the hope, the willing service—must be earnestly prayed for. While we see universal illustration of earthly gift-giving, why should we doubt the willingness and ability of our Heavenly Father to give us all we need? The Divine is richer than the human. The One who created all holds ever in His hand more than any creature can possibly claim title to. Of this great holding our blessing is born. But it is begotten of our faith. "Ask and ye shall receive," is the promise. The promise never fails. Perhaps it sometimes seems to, but 'tis only in the seeming. Each heart, with a faith in it, can say with PHŒBE CARY, that

—spite of many broken dreams,
This have I truly learned to say—
That prayers I thought unanswered once,
Were answered in God s own best way.

WHEN THE END COMETH.

HOWEVER careless-minded we may be, there will come in our soberer moments, questionings as to what awaits us when the end shall approach—the end of this little fragment of being which we call life. Just so sure as the days steal by, shall we come, sooner or later, to something new and strange, and of which we cannot fore-judge. We all feel this, more or less deeply ; and we all question within ourselves if we are ready to welcome this new and strange something into our lives. For we all believe that the end of which we speak is not really an end ; that there is more beyond ; that further away into the forever than we can conceive, our beings are to reach, —that there is no absolute death.

Men may drive away these questionings, in a measure, and may perhaps delude themselves for a time into the belief that they have to deal only with the present. But is it wise to do this? Is it prudent to say "Soul, take thine ease?" It is not doing away with the grave fact of the coming change. When the end cometh,—and the end, as we term it, will come,—we shall be obliged to face—what?

In our whole catalogue of words there is nothing like that brief " forever,"—brief, as a word ; longer than finiteness can measure; as a time. When the end cometh, the forever will begin. Here we can count upon nothing as lasting, but in that unending forever all things will be as unending as the forever itself. We shall joy on or sorrow on, with never a pause—never a summons to cease. Here we may be glad for a season and then sad for a season—the forever knows neither season nor change. Here we may do evil, if we will, and satisfy conscience by a promise of better deeds by-and-by,—in the forever we must reap the bitter fruits of our evil-doing, or the sweet rewards of doing well. Ah, that incomprehensible forever ! There are men whom the word haunts like a very demon,—men whose living is blackened by sin and crime ; who pretend utter recklessness of the future, but in whose mind the little word echoes and re-echoes like a never-dying reproach.

And there are others who whisper it sweetly to them-

selves—for whom it is the refrain of a song that makes
music in their hearts from morning until evening.   To
them it is suggestive of eternal gladness.   Their full acceptance of salvation through CHRIST makes of the forever, for them, a long Sabbath of Rest.   They feel that
when the end cometh, there will also come Peace.

When the end cometh. —It may be next year, or next
week, or—to-morrow.   It cannot be far off, at the most.
It may be nearer than we think ; our short to-day may
even now be illuminated somewhat by the light of the
never-ending to-morrow.   Only a little while, and we
shall greet the end which is but the beginning, and shall
take into our life an eternal joy or sorrow.

GOD'S MORROW.

O GOD ! in the night of my sorrow
Shine Thou with the light of Thy morrow !—
That day of sweet rest for the weary, of peace for the troubled
ones sore—
That day of glad sunlight so cheery,
Whose smile on the world-desert dreary
Shall quicken rare buds to their blooming, in beauty of bloom
evermore.

I wait, in the dark, its appearing,
Impatient the while it is nearing,
For, e'en though the stars may be shining, uncertain and dim is
the way ;

Perplexities past my divining
My feet from the path are inclining,—
I follow my Saviour like Peter, and go even further astray.

O God ! the dim twilight is chilling !
Send soon Thy bright morrow, all thrilling
With warmth that shall melt me to loving intenser, unshadowed
by fear !
I long for faith's full-fruited summer,
With doubting no more an incomer,
The sunshine of peace all about me and Jesus the Christ ever near!

"AS THE LEAF."

"WE do all fade as the leaf." Thus the soul whispers.
And mayhap the soul sighs a little, and looks back to
the bud and the blossom with somewhat of regret. For
fading is sad. And yet if fading be fulfillment, then it is
not sad. Has not the leaf fulfilled its mission? All
through the summer it has drunk the tree's juices, draw-
ing them up through the tree's wonderful cells that the
tree might grow and work out its destiny. Now its labor
is over. The growing time lapses into patient waiting.
Then what can the leaf do but fade?—fade gracefully, as
becomes a goodly leaf whose fulfillment is attained.

So if we all *do* "fade as the leaf," it is a blessed fading.
If we fade because our mission is wrought out, our labor
all ended, our opportunity filled full, surely there can be

no more glorious conclusion. In our sober second thought we question, Do we ? No leaf drops from its stem in this bright autumnal season, which, as a leaf, has not done its perfect work. Alas ! how many human leaves drop down to dust with their work all unwrought, their opportunity all unimproved, their mission a failure !

HUMAN SYMPATHY.

"One touch of nature makes the whole world kin." It is as true now as ever it was. Forget it often as we may, the fact will find its reminder in some hour we think not. A new life warms within when love is born. That new life thrives and grows when love abides ; and human love, which was born with our humanity, will abide while its existence is recognized and approved. With its abiding, abide better times for all mankind.

Such human love strengthens our love for things divine. We can trust GOD more completely when we put large faith in our fellows. Our hearts broaden toward Deity when they reach out widely to embrace the world. That man's Christianity ought to be best, whose humanity is most far-reaching. And so this is the precious lesson of a great woe : we *are* brothers all, at the last. We have common affections, and, thank GOD ! common hopes. And knowing all. sympathizing with us in all, we have an elder Brother, even JESUS CHRIST, in whose humanity we see an example for every human being, in whose divinity is our sure promise of that which is to come.

A PSALM OF PRAISE.

O'ER all November's dreariness,
    And all the waning year's complaint,
        Through smoky haze
        Of summer days
        That fill the skies
        With sweet surprise
    When earth in splendid vesture lies,
There comes a peace my soul to bless,
    And calm me, though I inly faint.

It steals upon me like a dream,—
    A tender dream, as softly kind
        As ever blest
        A soul at rest ;
        And one by one
        Each morning sun
    Is kissing me, as it has done
With magic in its golden beam
    Since Youth its garlands for me twined.

I live again each morning o'er ;
    I breathe again each morning's air,
        Each fancy sweet
        Again repeat ;

Each gladsome thrill
At dreaming's will
Asserts that it has power still ;
And joys that long have gone before
Another yield of pleasure bear.

Where I had sung a psalm of praise,
Again the praiseful psalm I sing ;
Where sad I sighed,
Or moaning cried,
I sigh no more
With sadness sore,
But know the fruit that sorrow bore
Is blessing all my brief to-days,
And so a peal of joy I ring !

As one by one the days go by,
I see my Lord's dear presence near :
His touch I feel
In woe and weal,
And day by day
He leads my way,
From morning till the evening gray ;
And gladly thankful then am I
To hear His voice of holy cheer.

I bless Thee, O Thou righteous God !
That yesterdays Thou gavest me !
That they were mine,
And I was Thine !
And Thee I bless
In thankfulness
For the to-day that I possess :
And when the way of life I 've trod
May I the past recall with Thee !

THE RENDERING OF GRATITUDE.

HERE on this Sabbath evening. which with its holy silence waits upon the New Year's dawning, what is more
fitting than that we think of all GOD has done for us in
the twelve-month gone, of all He may do for us in the
time to come? What more becometh us than heartfelt
gratitude for all His mercies?

But is the rendering of gratitude so simple a thing?
Is it indeed, so universal a thing? Grateful, are we?
Very likely; but not always in the way we should be.
As gratitude is a personal rendering, so should the rendering be to a personal GOD. It is not enough that we
feel a sort of gratitude to nature, to law. In nature and
in law we must see a living GOD,—a GOD of love and to
be loved,—and to Him must be rendered the service of
our hearts.

The beginning or the ending of any year may be really
no more than other times to us, yet it is well that we
consider such beginning or ending as a way-mark in life,
a sort of stopping place, where we may pause to look
back—where, in the midst of all our hurry and worry,
we may stop to be glad. For we are too rarely glad.
Those things which would cause regret and sorrow seem
to us far more numerous than those other things whereof
we should rejoice. But full to overflowing of happy happenings is our life, all the rounded weeks.

Happenings? Call them not so. There is no chance with Him to whom we owe all that we have and are. Nothing merely happens, with GOD, therefore nothing merely happens with us. We may use the word, if only we use it with the right meaning underneath. And because there is no happening—because all that comes to us of being and having is wisely foreordered—our gratitude should go out perpetually.

BLESSED ARE THEY THAT MOURN.

" BLESSED are they that mourn ! "
   Ah, many there be, then, blest !
No day its beauties complete hast worn
   Till evening lighted the West.
Some hour grows dark with woe
   Though bright soever the dawn,
Some bitter regret each heart must know
   For treasures too early gone.

We sorrow, alas ! how much !
   Our eyes grow weary of tears,
As pain comes closer with cruel touch
   Through all the pitiless years.
We sorrow, and weakly trust
   Through sorrow we may grow strong,
Yet sorrowing pray to the Good and Just—
   " How long, O our Lord, how long ? "

There comes to our human cry
    Response that is all divine,
And whether we heed it, or pass it by,
    ' T is equally yours and mine.
As sweet as a psalm of peace
    It echoes along the air,
And grief has ever its full surcease
    In this one answer to prayer.

How long shall we mourn ? Alas !
    The answer has naught of this ;
The night of our sorrow may quickly pass,
    Soon pain may be turned to bliss ;
Or never may come the dawn,
    And peace to the throbbing breast,
We never may chance on the gladness gone,—
    But they that do mourn are blest !

This, this is the answer heard
    In response to our human cry ;
God breathes no tenderer healing word
    To hearts that must hear or die.
Though sorrow has crushing weight,
    And leaves us bleeding and torn,
Reward for tears will be sweet and great,
    For "Blessed are they that mourn !"

"THERE could have been no silent Redeemer, and believe me, my friends, He can have no expressionless
representatives."

So said the preacher this morning, and to-night RUTH
calls up the saying, and we ponder it.

"Months ago," she remarks, "we read on one of our
Sabbath Evenings a poem about 'The Silent Christ.' I
shall always remember it. It spoke of the SAVIOUR's boy-
hood, and young manhood—of how He walked Judea's
hills and gave no sign of the divinity within Him—and
always since then I have seen at times the picture that
poem drew of my Redeemer's silent years. It must have
been a true picture ; and yet the preacher did not declare
amiss. CHRIST was not silent after His redeeming mission began. All His life then was just a wonderful
speech. How men listened to it ! How they are listen-
ing still ! "

"But if His followers be not voiceless," one asks, "do
they echo their Master's speech ? "

"Not often enough," is her answer. How can they ?
They are not divine. They are very human. They
speak out of human difficulties, and human besetments,
and the ten thousand surroundings that annoy and per-
plex. They are fretted, and harassed, and borne down

Their tongues are led astray, and they utter sad complaints. Their lives are warped by evil, and give sad testimonies. But they do somehow give expression. They are not dumb. Representing CHRIST before men, they speak for Him or against Him, whether they will or no. And the world listens, moved for good or ill."

"Would it not be better if we were voiceless for CHRIST, since we can not always give testimony in a wise way?"

"No. We must learn the wisdom of testifying. We must seek to live right, that our expression may be helpful, and true to Christian faith. Ours is not a testimony of the lips—that amounts to little—but of the life, and this amounts to much. Though we be dumb as statues, we may speak so that many shall hear and heed. It was not in His words alone, marvelous and profound as they were, that CHRIST spoke loudest to those around Him. He was eloquent for humanity in every act. No tributes of speech could have so tenderly sanctified human being, with all its possibilities, as did He sanctify the same wherever He walked and wrought."

"But we can not do as He did?"

"Certainly not. We can not raise the dead,— saving dead purposes to live nobly and unselfishly, and dead resolves to be pure of common sins ; we can not heal the sick, and bless the blind, and make a present heaven for those of perfect faith. Yet we can imitate the Master's life, and thus in some faint degree echo His abiding speech. We can look at His modest denial of self, and be more unselfish. We can see how He loved men, and be more forbearing.   We can remember how He suffered for the world, and be more patient as in the world we are made to suffer.   We can see how He trusted in the very deeps of darkness, and be more trustful when clouds of trouble come."

Ah, yes.   We can give a truer testimony that CHRIST did well so to speak and die for us all.   And men will note it if we do, and will ask what such living speech can mean.

BEFORE   THE   SERVICE.

DEAR Lord and Master, Thou who went
    Apart from men so oft to pray,
Give me a calm and sweet content,
    Communing here with Thee to-day!

I leave the world of sin behind,
    I turn to Thee my eager face,
All that I want in Thee to find,
    Within this hallowed, holy place.

My poverty its need forgets:
    Before Thy will my longing fails ;
The mist of murmuring and regrets
    Beneath Thy loving smile exhales.

My sinful self no more I see :
    Forgot is all that I have been ;

The veil between my soul and Thee
Is lifted, and I enter in—

Within a holier than this—
The temple of Thy love divine—
And foretaste have of heavenly bliss,
And know that endless joy is mine !

IN SIGHT OF THE CITY.

THERE is an old legend of a soldier who journeyed to-ward Jerusalem, to make crusade against the heathen who held it. His hopes were high, and he went on bravely day by day, till looking from a mountain-top at length he saw the city's walls and gleaming roofs, and thought his victory near at hand. Bnt then he sickened, and there he died—died in sight of the glories he never should enjoy.

Are we not all journeying toward Jerusalem ? The Pilgrim's Iion Gate is before us each. It must open, if ever we pass through into the beauties beyond. Like the brave Crusader, we may die in sight of the city's walls—may, yes, we must. It is given none to reach the goal, except they yield up life. But we are more blessed in our pilgrimage than the soldier was in his. To him death came with stern pathos, at the end of all his hopes and aims. There was the city, gleaming in the cloudless sun, but he should not set his foot therein.   All his toils had been for naught.   For us, however, the city will smile a welcome, when we come in sight, and we shall know if we be but wise in time, that the curtain of death lets down between it and us only to rise on brighter glories when the Glad Day dawns.

"*LET NOT YOUR HEART BE TROUBLED!*"

" LET not your heart be troubled ! "
 No sweeter words of cheer
The Master spake for their dear sake,
 Whose love was full of fear.
" Lo, I am with you always ! "
 Glad thought of lonely ones ;
Through dreary way by night and day,
 The silvery sentence runs !

" Let not your heart be troubled ! "
 What troubleth thine, my friend ?
Do you not know that Christ can go
 No more to painful end ?
Do yot not feel His comforting
 Amid your trials all ?
No bitter loss by cruel cross
 Can on your loving fall.

" Let not your heart be troubled ! "
 The springs of life are sweet
If you but drink at the fountain's brink

That flows by Jesus' feet.
In Him the doubt of being
  Its full assurance knows ;
In Him all fret and fear are met
  By full and sweet repose.

SHALL   HE   BE   SAVED ?

WE read the other day of a man buried in a well.
The well was deep and he could not extricate himself.
Through a small opening beside the pump he could be
communicated with, and could secure a little fresh air,
enough to prevent suffocation.   How friends rallied to
save him !   Through all the neighborhood ran the cry of
danger to a life.   They worked with a noble will—rela-
tives, neighbors, and those to whom the victim was only
a man, in need of humanity's service.   They called to
him encouragingly, they plied shovel and pick, they forgot all else on that quiet Sabbath afternoon, but this
man's great need and their great obligation.   Again and
again, as his deliverance seemed at hand, did the earth
cave in once more, and bury him more completely ; again
and again did they bend all their energies to the generous task.   They sank a pipe to him, and forced air down
through it ; they built a curb, to prevent the earth from
pressing too heavily upon his head ; they toiled on, al-

most without thought of tiring, putting more and more of plan and system into their work, vieing with each other in doing man's duty to man.

The day waned, but still they rested not. The merchant, the minister, the professional man, labored right on through all those weary hours, side by side with the humblest toiler from the ditch. Before the great stress of that awful time all class conditions vanished. They were simply all men, loyal to a common manhood, and zealous in a common cause. Darkness came on, the long hours of night wore away; but yet they wavered not. Morning dawned, and still was their brother in peril, discouraged, faint, perhaps dying. Only one or two could labor, as the end was neared, and these at the risk of their own lives. All were exhausted with their waiting and their work. Then the fire-bell rang out its warning of danger. To property? Ah, no! to a human life! Fresh hands must toil that any hands might save.

And they did toil, as bravely as their fellows had done. They toiled, and they won. A few hours more and the man was saved—weak, bruised, half-unconscious, but *saved;* and from all hearts went up a great throb of joy, while cheers of victory rent the air.

Down in the pit of intemperance a man has fallen. He is somebody's father, somebody's husband, somebody's friend. Let the cry run through all the community. Let it set the bells of alarm to ringing; let humanity be aroused! Shall he be saved? Into deeper and more dangerous depths never man fell. If he get

out at all it must be by the help of friendly hands, and
the merey of GOD. Are your hands outstretched? Are
you answering the call? Will you forget self and selfish
interests, and toil freely for this brother in distress?—will
you save a soul? "Unto the least of these, my little
ones," said the Master. His words were very broad, and
they reach over and include all duty, and all doing.
Wherever there is human need, there must humanity go
to help and to save. They must answer for their sin, who
walk selfishly by on the other side.

THE LONELY LAND.

A LONELY land !
                        Beneath an Eastern sun
It sleeps in dreary peace till day is done.
Along the sandy reaches pilgrims go
From lands far-lying, searching to and fro
For signs of that old life the ages knew
When earth was young, and men their nurture drew
So free and pure it beat through cycles long
In patriarchal pulses firm and strong.

A lonely land !
                        Its mountains calmly lift
Their faces sunward, but they see no thrift
Upon their slopes, and hear no busy hum

From valleys busy.   To them seldom come,
As early came, the saintly devotees
With plaint and prayer their pain of soul to ease.
They sit in silence, in a silent land,
As if they waited some Divine command.

A lonely land !
　　　　　　As kingly and serene
Fair Tabor rises, looking o'er the scene,
The dreamy hushes round about it thrill
To no glad being ; Esdraelon is still
As if it never felt the heavy tread
Of conquering legions ; all the past is dead
To present seeing ; on the dreary plains
No hint of fading Yesterday remains.

A lonely land !
　　　　　　The slope of Olivet
Is haunted by a ghost of old regret,
And in its silence ever seems to wait
The echo of some footfall missed of late ;
The paths that climb the hills of Nazareth
Are dull and somber as the walks of death,
And Bethlehem looks out of sober eyes
On all the peace that round about it lies.

A lonely land !
　　　　　　Uncertain Galilee
Is always but a patient, lonely sea,
In storm or calm, and rests amid its hills
Remembering ever, with a thought that thrills
To sweeter murmurs, touch of Godly feet,
And words of Masterhood when fierce it beat,
And sighing always for the men who came
And swept its bosom in the Master's name.

A lonely land !

For out of it went Christ !
And time and need have never yet enticed
His glad returning.   Waiting till He come,
The sweetest speech of vale and hill is dumb ;
The deepest breath of holiest Mount is stirred
For longing ear no more by healing word ;
The silent peace of all this silent land
Re-echoes never a Divine command !

A lonely land !

And yet the solitudes
Are full and prescient with a Life that broods
Above the present, as it pulsing went
Throughout the past,—a Life that sweetly bent
To bear the world's great burden, bore it then
From vale to mountain–top, and gave to men
The Life Immortal, from the Crown and Cross,
And left them rich, though lonely for their loss !

LOOKING   BACKWARD.

As we sit here in the firelight, on this final evening of
December, a fair face hangs before us on the wall.   Behind us, looking down upon the paper as we write, is a
portrait of dear old WHITTIER, the Quaker poet, who
seems to be thinking of his *vis-a-vis* opposite, the sweet,
fair face with eyes turned sidewise into distance—as he

thought years ago of another imaginative form,—as the
"Angel of the Backward Look!"
For the ideal head that hangs above our desk is Retro-
spection ; and the meditative womanhood it pictures is
looking backward, as so much meditative womanhood
and manhood beside is looking backward, on the time
gone by.   Now while the year grows old, and we are so
soon to turn the last page of our life-volume and read
"Finis" again, what vision more fit than this retrospective one?

We have come a toilsome way, perhaps?   Then let us
turn and gaze upon it, with hearts a little saddened for
the hurts it gave us, and the weariness it knew.   We
have lost some tender things out of our days, may be?
Then let us muse upon them in that sweet, sad silence
which is too holy for speech.   We have stumbled
over the pitfalls of our own wild passions and desires,
perchance?   Then let us look back over failures, and
sore bruises, and grow stronger amid regrets.

This angel of the Backward Look may be best company for every one, if only what she sees shall be wisely
turned by us to our account.   She is a Presence certain
as the life within.   She may hide herself, often, but she
rarely quite forsakes.   She walks with us all, day by day,
even as the ideal face looks always away into the past,
here in the quiet of our peaceful home.   She is meant
to be—let us trust she is—an angel of blessing; if she
were to prove otherwise, some might come to think her
almost a fiend.

Men should sometimes turn and look back, that they

may find a clearer vision for the way before. These retrospective pauses in life are full of happy advantage,— or ought to be. Our to-day should be wiser for our yesterday ; our future should prove richer for our past. We need the recession of distance to judge wisely what we were and what we did. Impulse cools, passion lapses, prejudice dies out, error sees less blinded, every faculty of being trims itself for truer use. Our present can not be correctly known, until we put it from us, and view it retrospectively. There can be no perspective except as we have light and shade, and these will appear to everyone who looking backward dwells alike on sad and glad things, seeing equal grace in each.

AT EVEN-TIME.

O LORD ! the way is dark and lone :
    I grope about, uncertain long ;
No gladness that my life has known
    Flows forth in happy thrills of song.
My sky with gloom is dull and drear :
    No stars smile out with beauty bright ;
But through the dark these words I hear—
    " At evening time there shall be light ! "

My midday sun has hid his face,—
    I can not see the glory round ;
If God should seek me in this place,

And make to me no sign or sound,
I should not know His presence near,
    I should not wonder at the sight ;
But in this promise is my cheer—
    " At evening time there shall be light ! "

O Lord ! in weariness I pray
    That Thou wilt come and walk with me,
As Thou of old didst walk the way
    With shining face, that I may see !
Or give me patience, till appear
    Some cheering rays, to bide the night,
And let me never cease to hear—
    " At evening time there shall be light ! "

Life's little day will reach its close ;
    The dreary way will find an end ;
To worn and weary sweet repose
    Will come as comes the dearest friend.
O Lord ! I pray Thee, grant that this
    Shall be my song when comes the night,
And day's dark gloom fades into bliss—
    " ' T is evening time, and there is light ! "

www.ingramcontent.com/pod-product-compliance
Lightning Source LLC
Chambersburg PA
CBHW030125030726
47498CB00007B/2550